Gavin's Woman

A PSI Sentinel Novella

PSI Sentinels: Darkwater Guardians

Pamela Moran

PSI Sentinels: Guardians of the Psychic Realm
Extraordinary senses in a world full of danger.

Protectors and hunters, PSI agents lay their
abilities, sometimes their lives, on the line. They
defend and shield unwary victims against the
twisted underside of a psychic society bent on
exploiting an unsuspecting, mundane world.

Acknowledgements

M.A. Taylor, Stephanee Ryle and Janelle Denison
Thank you for your help, your support, but
mostly for your friendship.
Ladies, you're the best!

Brook Tucker and Adam Affrunti
Brook, you make an awesome Calea.
Adam, I couldn't have found a more
perfect Gavin.
Thank you both for making my venture into
cover photography so much fun.

Dedication

Warren, I'm thrilled to be your woman.

I love you.

Chapter One

RAIN BEAT HARD against the thick plate glass, floor to ceiling windows overlooking a wild and storm tossed Pacific Ocean. As dark as the early February afternoon appeared, the time might as well have been dusk.

A cold, miserable dusk.

The only person in the second floor lounge, except for the hotel's bartender who occasionally wandered through, Calea Fontaine cradled a fragile, porcelain cup of hot, herbal tea between her chilled hands. Aromatic, floral infused, steam wafted upwards. Heat seeped into her fingers, but the warmth only spread so far.

She shifted in the overstuffed, leather chair, spared a split-second glance for the fire that burned low in the fireplace to her right. Maybe she should have sat closer, could have absorbed a fraction of the heat.

Should haves. Could haves.

Possibilities gone.

Fractured.

Destroyed.

She lifted the teacup to her lips, blew across the surface. Let the flowery, almost spring like fragrance fill her nose before she sat the cup on the small table beside her chair.

Tea had sounded so wonderful such a short time ago.

A lot of things had sounded wonderful. Once. Funny how a few short, terrible months changed things. Changed her perspective. Changed her.

Lightning flashed outside the window. Thunder boomed.

Close.

She shivered then pulled her knees to her chin, braced the heels of her soft soled shoes on the edge of her chair, and wrapped her arms tight around her jean clad legs.

Would she ever be warm again?

A prickle sparked up her spine. An awareness.

That alertness tightened her muscles, caught her breath in her throat. *Breathe in, breathe out.* Not like she hadn't known he'd show up here. Eventually. She angled her head to the left, with her cheek against her knee, and swept her gaze towards the wide archway leading to the open hallway overlooking the lobby. To the man who stood with his hands splayed at his hips, his black trench coat open and pushed back.

Rain droplets glistened like diamonds scattered across the dark material covering his wide shoulders. A scowl marred that rugged face, and a storm as dark as the one assaulting the Pacific brewed in his grey eyes.

Gavin Dunbar.

Her one time lover. Her *soul-mate.*

At least according to their respective grandmothers, who, as world renowned seers of love, were rarely ever mistaken.

But soul-mate didn't mean easy nor did it mean forever.

She'd learned that one the hard way.

"Why are you here?" Her voice, rarely used these last few days in Oregon, rasped low against her ears.

His scowl deepened. "Looking for you."

The deep timbre of his speech, even irritated, pulled at her. Inside, her treacherous breath stuttered, squeezed her heart. Damn him.

Not that damning him did any good.

"You found me. Not all that hard since I'm sure Ben told you where to look." Her boss had some explaining to do about that one, even though she'd known, at some level, he'd tell. She pulled her gaze away from Gavin to stare out the rain splattered windows. "Now go away. I'm meditating, communing with the storm."

"Right." He strode into the room, stood a few feet away.

And damn this hyper-awareness. Of him. Of every damn thing about him.

"What are you conjuring now?"

She angled her head to meet his tight gaze. "You're here, aren't you?"

His mouth, that full, kissable mouth, firmed.

Had she conjured him? A part of her had known he'd show. Known he wouldn't be able to stay away.

There were issues to be dealt with, words needing to be said. But was she ready? Would she ever be?

"Leave me alone." Again she tore her gaze away to stare out the windows. "I don't need you here. I don't need looking after. And whatever line of bullshit you fed Ben, he doesn't need you here, either."

"I didn't come all this way, in this weather, to simply turn around and leave."

Neither did he deny the line of bullshit Ben was too sharp to fall for, regardless of anything else. "Your problem. Not mine."

"Calea —"

"I don't *want* you here."

"We don't always get what we want."

"Oh, I'm intimately familiar with that." She let sarcasm drip from her words, *felt* him stiffen. Too damn bad. He should've stayed away. Could've made different choices.

Back to should haves, could haves, and a heart she was no longer willing to risk.

"Callie?" A different male voice, not as deep but laced with concern, came from the archway.

Gavin turned to glare at the intrusion.

She lifted her head from her knees and let a small smile play over her lips as she deliberately ignored the man who still held all the pieces of her battered heart. "Yes, Roy?"

"Just making sure you're okay, Callie." The bartender's deep set, dark brown gaze shifted between hers and

Gavin's then back to hers. His broad shoulders squared and his chin lifted. "That you don't need anything."

"I'm fine." *Liar*. But she'd become good at denying her own internal issues. Wasn't that why she'd convinced Ben she needed to get away? Rest, relaxation. Reflection?

To decide if she was ever going back.

"Let me take that tea you're not really drinking." Roy moved further into the room. He shrugged his right shoulder, a jerky, almost apologetic move. "Would you prefer something else?"

Calea frowned. She hadn't drank any of the tea, much as she'd wanted it such a short time ago. The liquid was still warm, still drinkable, but at this point the thought of it turned her stomach. "No. I'm good, Roy."

With the fragile cup lost in his big hand, Roy stood next to her but his gaze locked on Gavin's. "Did you want something?"

Calea bit her bottom lip to keep her laugh contained at the barely concealed insolence in Roy's tone. *That* wasn't going to go over well with Gavin Dunbar, Government Liaison to the PSI, Ben Garrett's covert psychic agency, much less *Mr*. Dunbar, son of Senator Dunbar.

Gavin's eyebrow raised.

Roy's eyes narrowed.

"We're fine, Roy." She touched the man's arm, her fingertips barely grazing his shirt sleeve.

His eyelids fluttered, the movements small and almost unnoticeable. The same with the slight dip of his head. His gaze flicked to hers and he brushed her shoulder with the tip of his fingers. "You're sure?"

A troubled soul, a simple man. One she didn't see a future for. Not that he didn't have one, just one she couldn't *see*. Right now, she was okay with that. "Yes, I'm sure."

He nodded once, sent Gavin another short glare then met her eyes again. "I'm in the bar if you need anything, Callie."

A guardian of sorts. A care-taker.

Guaranteed to raise Gavin's ire. Piss him off.

She just wanted to be left alone.

Silence prevailed for a long, stretched out minute as Roy left and Calea again focused on the storm outside the windows.

"Callie?" A slight layer of derision coated Gavin's voice.

Without looking at him, she shrugged. "Ben's idea."

"Because it's close enough you'll remember to answer to it." A deep sigh rumbled from his broad chest. "Although you've been to this place how many times?"

Too many to count. Her refuge from the world, not that it helped now. "Ownership change. New management."

So technically, no one knew her. She'd been hell-bent on leaving, Ben hadn't wanted to risk her being found.

Gavin pulled another of the overstuffed, leather chairs closer to her before removing his coat and draping it across the back. Then he settled his big frame into the chair and leaned his head back. Another sigh escaped.

Still, she didn't quite look directly at him. "I didn't invite you here. I don't want you here."

"Calea." Exhaustion laced his low voice. "I am here. The soonest I can leave is tomorrow. I don't see any reason to rush back out into that storm simply because you object to my presence."

"*You don't see* is exactly the problem." She straightened, planted her feet on the floor and met his hooded gaze. "I'm assuming you already have a room."

He laced his fingers over his stomach.

"On my floor."

Just freaking wonderful.

"Fine." She stood. "There's a book calling my name and I believe I'll have room service for dinner. Since I won't see you before you leave, have a good trip home tomorrow."

GAVIN SAT WHERE Calea had left him, after she'd glided through the archway separating the second floor lounge from the open hallway overlooking the lobby, her head held regally high and without a backwards glance. He sat for a solid fifteen minutes.

Brooding.

Staring out the windows as rain pelted the glass.

She was a damn fool, out here alone. No protection. No one to watch her back.

While the threat to her safety was real. Substantiated. The fact several months had passed since that attempt didn't mean a damn thing. Milford was patient. He'd proven that more than once.

And the man wanted Calea.

Gavin would be damned himself before he let that happen.

In spite of whatever the hell Calea wanted.

THREE HOURS LATER, more comfortable in jeans and a white T-shirt, Gavin stood with his hands braced on either side of his seventh floor hotel room door and his eye pressed to the peep hole.

Damn Calea's prickly ass.

She'd said she was going to stay in her room and damned if she hadn't.

Being early February, with a series of storms hitting the coast, the hotel was practically empty. Add in the partial renovation and the place only needed a skeleton staff.

So, no issues acquiring the room directly across from Calea's.

Not that he'd expected any.

The unknown in all of this was Calea herself. Getting any kind of read on her had always been impossible for him.

He pushed away from the door, ran a hand over his face before pacing the length of the room. Again. His door was cracked open, he'd swung the inside door latch between the door and its frame, so he could hear any movement in the hallway.

Non-existent movement.

She was tucked in her damn room, probably curled in her chair with a book. Calm, collected and oblivious to the turmoil across the hall.

Turmoil with his name scratched all over it.

He paused, hands on hips, and glanced back at the door.

What had he expected?

Her to welcome him with open arms?

Fat chance.

He moved again.

At the wall of curtains covering the windows facing east and overlooking what, during the spring and summer, were the gardens, he eased back the heavy drapes. Rain still assaulted the glass, but it didn't seem as hard.

For now.

This storm was supposed to last well into tomorrow with another on its heels.

How appropriate.

What few lights he had on in the room flickered.

He dropped the curtain back into place, rummaged to the bottom of the suitcase he had open on the luggage stand and pulled out the long, thin black flashlight he kept packed there.

Being caught in the dark wasn't an option.

The smaller, also black, flashlight from his computer bag, he slipped into his back pocket. He left his gun tucked at the small of his back.

Again the lights flickered.

He glanced at the door, took several steps forward, and the lights went out.

Adrenaline tightened his stomach. Kicked his ass.

Shit.

Long flashlight in his left hand, he tore out of his room and across the hall.

"Calea." He banged the outside of his right fist against her door one time. "Open up, Calea."

Those few seconds screamed an eternity.

The metallic click of a deadbolt being released then the scrape of the latch being swung back eased a few of the bands constricting his chest. As the door inched open he shoved his way a foot inside the room.

Calea stood, one hand gripped around the door knob and the other around her own flashlight. She blocked his path into the room and stood her ground. "What the hell is wrong with you?"

"The lights are out." His gaze swept the room behind her.

No lights, but with the curtains shoved back and the windows fully exposed, a small amount of light cast shadows across the west facing room.

Although rain no longer hit the glass, dark, angry clouds still hung low with dusk no more than a thin smear of orange on the horizon.

"Probably the storm." She let go of the door knob and, with her flashlight held like a weapon, she crossed her arms over her chest.

"Probably." He stepped around her, fully entered her room. "Nice view."

Her room faced the Pacific, overlooked the cliffs. Anyone wanting to see in would have to be out on that ocean. And anyone trying to access the room through the wall of windows would have to use the window washing rig he'd spotted earlier in the parking garage, when he'd arrived.

Or a rope.

From the roof.

He could do it.

Even in the storm.

Especially in the storm.

No need to be as quiet. Less fear of being discovered.

Shit.

"Gavin."

"What?" He flicked on his flashlight, bounced the beam around the room.

"There's no one in here except me."

"And now me."

"And now you're leaving."

"Wrong, sweetheart."

"Bullshit."

He glanced at her then went back to prowling the room. The lights flickered on.

"See? Everything's fine. You can leave."

"I could." His heart no longer thudded in his chest, she was safe. But he was here, now, standing between her and the windows and he wasn't going anywhere. Since she wouldn't like it, she'd have to deal with it. His mouth twitched.

"Gavin." That layer of calmness, so much a part of her, slipped a fraction. "Don't you dare laugh at me."

"Wouldn't dream of it." That grin breaking across his mouth wasn't his fault. The chuckle either. *Blame the relief.*

Those gorgeous eyes of hers, whiskey brown right now, in the lower light, narrowed. She raised her flashlight and shook it at him. "This isn't funny."

Instantly sober, he nodded once. "Actually, it is. But only because you *are* safe."

"Gavin —"

"What?" He settled in one of the wingback chairs in the small sitting area a few feet from the partially opened bedroom door. In there, on the other side of that door, was a perfectly made up king-sized bed. *That* he studiously ignored. He wasn't here to indulge his addiction to her soft, pliable body. Those days were over. Done. In the past.

Had to remember that. To remind himself of that.

He folded his hands over his stomach.

She stared at the ceiling with a look of *give me strength.* His cheek twitched.

So he enjoyed provoking her. *Sue me.*

"Gavin —"

A knock on the door stopped her. She angled her head towards the sound as Gavin straightened in his seat, his hand behind his back on the butt of his gun.

"Callie?" Roy, the disingenuous bartender, called out through the still partially opened door. "I have your room service."

Gavin tucked his gun under his thigh and leaned back in the high backed chair, again folded his hands over his stomach while he mentally sifted through what he'd read in the file Ben had compiled on the hotel and its employees.

Roy Hoffman. There hadn't been much on him. He'd been hired less than two months ago. A relative of a local resident, Roy was house sitting while his great aunt and uncle took an extended trip to Europe.

Nice guy. Helpful nephew.

On the surface.

Roy, pushing the door further open, leaned into the room.

Gavin widened and broadened the top level of his senses to the man.

Not intruding on the man's space. Simply open to what was out in the ether. What the man, himself, emitted.

Murky layers of negative energy undulated around Hoffman, gloomy wisps of dim fog defied definition. Not that Gavin *saw* the layers or even *felt* them. Some would say he *read* a person's surface but he couldn't describe the whole process as anything more than *knowing*. And right now, what he *knew* was Roy Hoffman was bad news.

Gavin allowed a superior smile to hover over his mouth as Hoffman's gaze swept the room. That gaze widened then narrowed as it hit Gavin.

An answering echo vibrated through the air, sucked the oxygen from the room. From Gavin's lungs.

Shit. Bad intentions.

Partially unformed and suddenly, instantaneously changed.

The tenuous connection snapped. Dank air rushed back in, filled the empty crevices. Coated the room, Gavin's lungs.

Helpful nephew, my ass.

He pressed his thigh down on his gun, the reassurance of its presence calming him.

He'd take the bartender out, risk his own life, before he'd allow the man anywhere near Calea.

She wasn't going to be hurt. Wasn't going to happen. Not on his watch.

Chapter Two

TENSION STRETCHED AS Gavin held Roy Hoffman's gaze across the expanse of Calea's hotel room. From the hallway, the bartender leaned in but stayed behind the partially closed door.

Seconds ticked by.

Gavin's gun, tucked under his thigh on the wingback chair where he sat, warmed. His fingers, laced over his stomach, itched.

Give me a reason.

Hoffman's gaze flicked between Gavin's and to where Calea stood, completely still, several feet away. Then back to Gavin.

I only need one reason.

"I don't think there's enough dinner for two, but I could bring something else up, if that's what you want." Hoffman, his tone insolent, shoved the door open further, turned to the food service cart behind him and tugged on the handle. He stumbled forward, yanking the cart sideways. His knees hit the ground, the cart hit the door and dishes rattled against each other.

Calea took two steps.

"Cal —" Gavin, not moving, bit off her name. "Callie. Stop."

She did and glanced at him over her shoulder. Nodded once and actually backed up those two steps she'd taken then moved to the side, giving him a direct line of sight to the door.

Good girl.

Excellent training.

Roy pushed himself to his feet, wiped at his knees then straightened. A red flush stained his cheeks. One that matched the thick stain spreading across the white cloth covering the top of the room service cart. He glanced at the mess, twisted his face in a semblance of a groan then, avoiding Gavin's gaze, shrugged one shoulder as he focused on Calea. "I spilt your soup."

"Accidents happen." Her voice held that soothing calmness that made her such a great instructor back at the Institute. A quality that had her students so willing to give her all they had in them, to not disappoint her.

"I was stuck in the elevator when the power went out. I guess I'm more shaken than I'd thought." Roy wiped a hand down his pant leg and backed up a step. "I'll bring you another bowl."

"Add a burger and well-done fries to that." Gavin let his chin touch his chest but kept his gaze leveled at the man.

Calea raised her own gaze to the ceiling then back to Roy. "That does sound good. How about we forget the soup and change it to two burgers, but only one order of fries."

"Nothing to drink?"

"We have the coffee maker, so we're fine." Gavin flicked a glance at Calea.

"And I have plenty of coffee."

Roy's frown deepened but he nodded and backed the cart out of the room.

Once the man was gone Gavin waited several more moments.

Not a hardship considering Calea stood with her fists on her hips, her dark hair in that thick braid swung over one shoulder and her head back while she counted to ten. Or maybe twenty. Whatever the number, she made a pretty picture. All pissed off at him.

On a deep intake of breath she faced him, one eyebrow raised and that soft mouth in a straight line. "What was the purpose of that?"

"The man is a klutz."

"You make him nervous."

"Why would that be?"

"Because –" She wrapped her arms around her middle, swung her gaze to her door which hadn't completely closed. "Your door is still cracked open. Do you have your key?"

He nodded. Guess she'd caught the little fact he was directly across the hall. Not that he'd been hiding it.

She spun on her heel, made short work of securing his door while he called down to the front desk to request the chef himself bring their food up this time.

While he normally didn't like to flaunt his position, in this instance he had no qualms.

Calea arched one brow before easing her own door closed and securing the locks.

He had no illusions about her wanting him in her room, but for now she wasn't pressing the issue. Small favor, one he'd take right now.

A few feet into the room she stopped, set one hand on her hip and pointed a finger at him. "So, why do you make Roy so nervous?"

"Maybe it's simply a male thing?"

"Sure. And I'm the Queen of England."

He bowed his head. "Your highness."

She fisted her hand. "Don't make me drag it out of you."

"Could be fun."

Her head came up and a spark of pure anger lit her eyes.

An answering flare of instant, pure lust flamed inside him. Sick bastard that he was. His *want* of her always there, just under the surface, ready to ignite, incinerate and leave behind nothing more than simmering ashes.

Such was his passion for Calea Fontaine.

And such was the reason he buried it as deeply as possible.

Otherwise all that would remain of either of them would be cold cinders. Useless for anything or anyone else.

"What did you get off him?" Her voice tight, she settled in the other chair at an angle from him with a small round table between them.

Distance, even that small amount, was an excellent thing.

Roy. The nefarious bartender. He was the question, wasn't he? Gavin rubbed a hand over his face. "Nothing specific. Bad intentions. Not even sure they're fully formed."

"You, of all people, know that lots of people have bad intentions. Nebulous, ugly thoughts you pluck out of the ether." Her small, soundless, sigh washed over him as she settled against the back of her chair and folded her hands across her lap. "How many actually act on them?"

"Cut the condescending attitude, Queenie." He arched an eyebrow. "I'm not one of your students."

Her mouth tightened at that. And her eyes narrowed.

Good. *Keep her pissed, give him something* different *to focus on.*

"And maybe you were a hundred percent right when you said it was a male thing." The edges of her mouth lifted in a non-smile. "Posturing, preening and projecting territorial rights where there are none."

His own eyes narrowed.

"No wonder Roy turned into such a klutz."

"And maybe he's the one posturing and feeling threatened by my presence because he's one of those with every intention of acting on those bad intentions. With you at the forefront of his mind, at the first opportunity."

That dark gaze of hers, still shadowed in this light, locked on his. She angled her head to the right, slightly, and moss green glinted in the depths of her eyes. "So that's what you're picking up?"

Weariness, right there all day, ebbed to the surface, swamped him. He leaned back to rest his head against the high back of the chair. Nodded once. "Yeah."

"But you're not picking up any links, any ties to Milford?"

"No. Nothing quite as formed as that." He closed his eyes, concentrated on the *sense* he'd picked up off the bartender. Opened his eyes a crack, caught her troubled gaze. "Nebulous is a good word. I'm not able to get a good read on the man's actual intent. Seems he hasn't quite decided yet, but there's something there. Something that says he wants to hurt you."

"Oh."

"Yeah."

"That's why Ben sent you?" She ran her hand down the length of her braid, fingered the end of the green ribbon threaded through her hair. "Because he picked something up after all?"

Gavin dropped his gaze. *Treacherous ground here.* The *why* of the why the hell *was* he here? Ben had readily given him the information of Calea's location. Had almost made it *too easy.* "Something like that."

"Dammit." She rubbed at the back of her neck but her words held no heat. "Ben gave me up without a fight, didn't he?"

Gavin met her puzzled gaze. At least she wasn't really pissed about it. Yet. "He had his reasons."

"Did he give you any ideas about those reasons?"

"No. But since he always has one, we really need to be on guard."

"Why didn't he simply call me home?"

"Maybe it's as nebulous as Roy's intentions."

"So he didn't say it was Milford?"

Gavin shook his head. He and Ben hadn't actually discussed much. Gavin had shown up, unannounced, at the Institute, demanded to know where the hell Calea was and Ben had handed over the address to this place along with the corporate jet's departure time from the little airport south of the Institute.

Ben wasn't clairsentient, but any number of people at the Institute might have had a glimmer of trouble. Clairsentience was one of the hardest psychic skills to control. To decipher. To utilize.

To understand.

Gavin got that. Most of the agents got that. Hell, even the director of Homeland Security got that.

Didn't make Gavin happy, though. Made him edgy, with the spot between his shoulder blades tight. Made him feel manipulated. Like his decisions weren't his own, were out of his control.

Made him pissed. "Didn't say it wasn't Milford, either."

"Ben's a law unto himself. What I don't understand is what Milford could possibly want with me." A frustrated sound vibrated low in her throat. "We only have one ex-student's word Milford was even involved."

"One *dead* ex-student."

"Yes." Sadness laced the word. "*Why?* I'm not some super spy. I don't have over the top psychic skills. I'm basically a teacher."

"Maybe Milford's looking for love and needs you to tell him where to look." He shouldn't goad her, he knew that.

Daggers direct from her eyes speared right through his heart. He could *feel* the icy tip of each one, piercing his skin. Twisting. Not that he didn't deserve each and every one. Didn't make that cold glare any easier to take, however.

The lift of her lips matched the chill in her eyes. "Like you believe in prophecy."

Oh, he believed. Just had no intentions of letting it run him. Or ruin their lives. "My belief isn't necessary. Only Milford's. And if he does believe, you're descended from the best. You're Mimi Fontaine's granddaughter."

"Let's ignore the fact I'm not nearly as skilled as Mimi, nor do I embrace the ability. And none of that is enough to kidnap someone over. To kidnap me."

"For Milford, it might be enough. And that *one, ex-student?* Someone killed Tommy, took him out. To keep him from talking would be my guess."

Calea looked away, out the dark window.

Dusk had completely fallen, leaving everything outside as black as the darkest night.

"If he's not after you for himself, maybe he believes you have something to offer to Milford Enterprises."

"What, though?"

"Why did Tommy leave the Institute?"

She stayed silent for so long, Gavin wondered if she was going to answer him. Then, her sigh quiet, she shook herself. "Strong, natural talent but balked hard at having to discipline himself."

"But you got through to him. If I remember correctly, he sang your praises to anyone who would listen."

Her head came up and she met his gaze.

So maybe he'd been all too willing to listen. He wasn't apologizing for that.

Instead, he stayed silent and held her gaze.

Another small sigh escaped her. "Yes, I got through to him. That rock-climbing wall we installed in the gym helped his focus. From there, he seemed to gain an understanding of his talent, of how to lessen its control of his emotions, his life."

"And he was grateful."

She nodded.

"But not enough to stick around."

"The Institute isn't for everyone."

"Neither are the PSI."

Her eyes narrowed. She'd gone through the agency program. Had worked in the field. Had hated every moment of it. Gavin knew that. Knew Ben hadn't wanted to lose her and had created her current position on the Institute side. He also knew she'd made that position her own and was now an invaluable asset to the Institute.

But she was strongly considering leaving.

She hadn't said it, hadn't actually told Ben – at least not that he'd shared – but a person didn't need Gavin's ability to read the intent that hung thick in the air surrounding them.

"Why are you here, Gavin?"

Good question. "A friend is in need. In danger. What other reason do I need?"

"So I'm a *friend*, now?" Her chin came up. "How ... chivalrous of you."

Dammit. "Calea, I'm not giving in to my grandmother's manipulations. Not anymore. But that doesn't mean I don't care about you. About what happens to *you*. Or that I won't do everything in my power to protect you. To keep you safe."

"Safe from everything and everyone except *you*."

Dammit, rehashing his decisions wasn't why he was here. She *knew* his reasons as well as he did. He held her gaze, refused to look away. "What is it you want me to say?"

"I don't want you to say *anything*. I want you to leave me alone."

At the absolute conviction in her voice, the air in his lungs stilled, thickened, threatened to turn to stone. They had no future together, but a future without her in it scared the crap out of him. Irrational. Stupid. "Calea –"

"None of this explains what Milford, or even Milford Enterprises, wants with me. Or why he would go to such lengths to try and kidnap me. It's been months. You're being paranoid."

So they were back to that and their *discussion* was over.

He wasn't sorry. "It's paranoia to want to keep you safe? That kid died because –"

"Of me?" Guilt mixed with the pissed off daggers she aimed at him. "Is that what you're saying?"

"No." Shit, how had this disintegrated this far? This fast? He wiped a hand over his face. "He died because someone was coming after you. We don't know the kid's part in it. Whether he was trying to protect you or set you up. Either way, his death is on whoever was behind it. Not you."

"Then why –"

"I'm scared. For you. For your safety. For your life."

Her turn to hold his gaze. No blinking. "Gavin. My safety is not your concern. My life is not your responsibility."

His jaw tightened.

"You can't have it both ways."

"How is worrying about an extremely real threat to your life having it both ways?"

"I can't handle this, Gavin. I can't be your *friend*. I can't sit here and pretend our past never happened. And I can't live and work in a place where you feel so free to drop in on a whim and disrupt my life on a constant basis."

There it was. Out in the open.

How the hell did he hit rewind? "The Institute is my job."

"Which is why I'm not going back."

"Calea –"

"No, Gavin." She pushed up from her chair, paced the length of the room before she turned to face him. "I'm not going back."

"But the risk of being away from there —"

"Isn't your problem."

Dammit. How the hell could she be so obstinate about her own safety? That sick sinking in his gut? He tried to ignore that. "If you're asking me to stand aside and let someone hurt you, it's not happening."

Over his dead body.

A sound, a light scraping against the outside of the door, echoed soft through the room. Pulling his gun from under his thigh, he shoved to his feet.

"Dinner?" Calea's voice, low and full of caution, matched the look in her eyes as she met his gaze.

"Maybe." He held up a hand. She didn't want his protection? Tough shit. She had it anyway. He listened.

They both listened.

Nothing for several moments, then a firm knock on the door. "Dinner is here."

Gavin shared a glance with Calea. The chef. Not Hoffman.

The tension in Calea's shoulders eased. Gavin tucked his gun away, straightened his shirt over it and moved to open the door.

Deal with the food first, Calea's stubbornness later.

Then there would be the sleeping arrangements.

Chapter Three

WITH THE REMNANTS of their dinner and the serving cart outside Calea's hotel room door, she ran a hand down her braid and fingered the ribbon tied at the end. Gavin, settled in the wing-backed chair he seemed to have made his own, folded his hands over his stomach and aimed that devastating smile her way.

But she wasn't falling for that. Not anymore. She had a couple of questions for him and then it would be time for him to head back to his room.

Alone.

"So." She sat forward in her own chair, braced her hands on the cushion under her thighs. "Tell me what else you think about Roy."

"What makes you think I picked anything else up from our not so friendly bartender?"

"Come on, Gavin. You've formulated ideas. Have theories."

"I do."

"And?"

"The wheels are turning inside him. His intentions aren't quite formed. Not fully. He's pissed that I'm here, in your room." Gavin's eyes narrowed, unfocused for a few moments. "The soup was a problem. That's why he spilt it."

"How so?"

"Not really sure." He shrugged, ran a hand over the top of his head. "Maybe he put something in it."

She frowned. "Why didn't you pick that up when he was here, in the room?"

"That's part of what's bothering me. If he did put something in your soup, why the hell didn't I *know*?"

"You picked nothing up at all?"

"Not a damn, specific thing. Nothing beyond hazy, negative nastiness."

Her lips pressed together, she stared at the floor and mentally traced a pattern in the carpet.

Gavin was very much a man of the present. His talent dwelt in the now, not in possibilities or vague maybes, but in actualities. In decisions made.

While the past might have bearing on a person's intent, Gavin couldn't – or didn't – pick up the 'what' or 'why'. And as far as the future, it was too tenuous, undefined, too fluid and therefore not to be trusted. At least as far as he was concerned. Which was part of why he didn't trust predictions or those who made them.

Like both their grandmothers.

Like her.

"But Hoffman putting anything in your soup is pure conjecture on my part." Gavin shook his head. "I'm guessing he hasn't quite given up that idea."

"So you truly believe he's trying to poison my food?"

"Maybe." Irritation mingled with the frustration lining his voice. "Or maybe it's something like a date-rape drug. I don't know. Not for sure. It's like he's waiting for me to get out of the way and you to have something liquid again. Something he can hide *something* in. Then he'll decide what he's going to do."

"Which is why you insisted on the chef bringing up our dinner." A chill coalesced into a hard knot right at the dead center of her stomach. "Does it have to be liquid to be able to hide something?"

"No, but that seems to be his focus so maybe it's easier for him."

A knot tightened in her chest. Roy was a problem, after all. Gavin was right. No matter how badly she'd wanted to dismiss his concerns. "My tea, earlier, was still hot."

"But he insisted on taking it away." Gavin's gaze sharpened. "My appearance must have changed his mind."

"That would explain why he seemed scattered to you. Unfocused."

His eyes narrowed as he frowned. "I never said he was scattered."

"But you think he is."

"Yes." His frown deepened. "Are you able to read me, now?"

"No." She waved a hand, shook her head. "Don't be ridic –"

"What else?"

"Nothing." *Go away.*

"Calea."

A glimmer, softly golden, glittery and not quite there, flitted at the edge of her vision. *No, this can't be right. I can't be reading his future.* How was that even possible?

She *couldn't* read Gavin. Because if she could, that meant – She pressed her fingers to her temples. Shook her head. "You need to go back to your room, Gavin."

Before I make an utter fool of myself.

"I'm not going anywhere."

"You paid for that damn room. You should use it."

"Probably. Not going to."

"Gavin –"

"Calea." He smiled, although his eyes held that trace of concern that had always been part of her undoing. Damn him. He spread his hands. "What's the purpose of me being here if I'm going to leave you unprotected at night, when you're at your most vulnerable?"

"I told you, I'm not your responsibility."

"And I don't give a damn what you told me."

"That's your problem." She needed him gone. "I have a lock on my door. I'm fairly decent at shielding."

Go away.

"Right now, Hoffman is *our* problem. With me here, we both *know* you will be fine."

Arrogant bastard. Why did he have to be right?

"And tomorrow we'll head for the airport and then back to the Institute."

"So you can deliver me into Ben's care?" Maybe she was being bitchy, she didn't care anymore. "So you can wipe your hands of me while you pat yourself on the back for helping a *friend* in need before you head home to D.C.?"

Gavin's mouth tightened.

"I'm not going back to the Institute."

"Why don't we talk about this in the morning?"

"Fine. Whatever." With an insincere smile aimed in his general direction, she pushed herself out of her chair. At her bedroom door, she paused, but only for a moment. "Sleep well."

Once the door clicked closed behind her, forming a solid barrier between them, she leaned against it and scrunched her eyes closed against the moisture pooling behind her lids.

Dammit. In all these months she hadn't yet cried over him. Dammed if she was going to start.

She wiped her hands over her face, shoved away from the door.

He thought he was so *freaking* smart. That his future was *his* and his alone. That *he* got to make all the decisions on his own terms. Not their separate grand-mothers' terms or even hers.

He'd insisted on directing his own life, calling his own shots. His own future.

With no regard to her or her future.

His decisions.

The image she'd seen earlier, that golden glimmer again hovered at the edge of her vision. She didn't know exactly what it meant for Gavin, but she was afraid of what it meant for her.

Gavin Dunbar had put both their lives on hold and had somehow, someway, changed the future after all.

And she was the only one in on the irony.

That, if she were still here, still alive, she'll be forced to *see,* in prophecy, Gavin Dunbar with someone else.

A *different* woman. A *different* soul-mate.

GAVIN SAT IN the wing-backed chair where Calea had left him a few minutes before and leaned his head back. She'd *read* him and it freaked her out.

Hell, it freaked him.

She shouldn't be able to *read* him. Read his thoughts, concerns about Hoffman.

Not only because of the damnable *soul-mate* connection, but reading someone in that way wasn't – hadn't – been one of her gifts. Ever. So, why now? Why him? Why here?

Thunder boomed off in the distance.

The storm's next wave was heading in, would soon be pounding the shoreline.

He didn't have the skill set, the talent, to set shields, although he could *feel* Calea's like an itch he couldn't quite scratch. Just out of reach, pressing on him, tightening his chest like air too heavy to breath.

No. Shielding wasn't his thing. But he had his gun, a chair facing the door, and an ability to sleep like a cat.

No one would be hurting her tonight.

GAVIN, HIS EYES opened in mere slits, widened his senses to test the perimeter of Calea's hotel suite.

Through the window, at a forty-five degree angle from where he sat in the wing-backed chair, dawn came in dismal, grey streaks across a still dark sky.

Nothing stirred.

Even the rain seemed to pause and hold its breath.

Something had prodded him, tapped on his senses. Woke him.

Hoffman?

No. Not Hoffman. Or at least not a hundred percent Roy.

Focus.

Calea's shields were firm. Not breached.

Not as thick as his mother's had always been, but there pressing against him.

Didn't matter a damn bit that Calea had anchored them in the suite's walls. They still kept his throat tight, his gut churning.

He rolled his shoulders, sucked air into his heated lungs then lifted a hand as he pushed his senses beyond the suite's boundaries. Beyond Calea's shields.

Not at the top of his skill-set, but he could perform in a pinch.

Nothing, though. Nothing tangible. Nothing he could grab and decipher.

Just as nebulous as Hoffman's bad intentions.

Dammit.

Awareness, a different kind, skittered across his skin.

Calea was awake.

On a burning, outward breath, Gavin let go of his impromptu probe and straightened. He wiped a hand over his face then pasted a half smirk over his mouth as the door to her bedroom opened.

Standing there, with her hair loose around her shoulders, the dark green of her night shirt accenting the shades of the forest in her sleepy, changeable eyes, she blinked several times before her gaze cleared and sharpened. "What was that?"

"What did it feel like?" He shifted in his seat. Why the hell did just the sight of her go straight to his groin?

"So you did feel it, too." She ran her fingers through her hair, shook the wavy mass out.

Man, she was killing him. On too little sleep.

"Almost like one of those alarm clocks with the soft, gentle tones. The kind meant to wake you slowly. Easily."

"Yeah. Like an easy tap on the shoulder." He watched as she moved to the window then stood there, arms crossed over her middle, and stared at the water. "Ben?"

"Your guess is as good as mine on that one." She shrugged both shoulders. "But, really, calling is more his style."

"Technology is his friend."

"Did you pick up anything with your probe?"

He'd known, on some level, she'd feel that. Her shields were good where his were practically non-existent. But then – he pressed his thigh down, on his gun – technology was also *his* friend. "Nothing tangible."

"Good? Bad?"

He shook his head. "Not bad, but I don't have anything to hang that on."

"Going with your feelings, your gut, isn't a bad thing, Gavin." She tilted her head to meet his gaze.

"Absolutes are better."

"Hmmm." She turned back to the window. "Whatever it was, it wanted us awake. Both of us."

That part he got. "Since we are, why don't we get the hell out of here?"

She nodded. "I need thirty minutes to shower and pack."

"I'll make coffee."

"Or you can head over to your room and get yourself ready to leave."

Stubborn woman. "Or I can wait until you're done so you can stand guard over me."

"I'm not standing guard over you."

"Then we can shower together." He let a wicked smile play over his mouth. "Be done in half the time."

Or not done for hours.

His groin tightened more.

Her, naked with him in the shower. *Hot* didn't cover where those thoughts took him.

If she didn't kill him first.

Her eyes narrowed, she turned on a bare heel and walked away from him. He watched the soft sway of her hips until she slammed the bedroom door between them.

He leaned his head back against his chair.

What would he have done if she'd called his bluff?

Resisting her was *his* option. His decision. And that was damn difficult.

Like an addict, when he was around her, all he wanted was *her*. Her arms around him, her legs around his waist. Her body pressed tight against his. Her scent filling him.

He'd tried to stay away.

Couldn't.

Ass of the first order.

However, with Hoffman lurking nearby and Milford out there somewhere, Gavin wasn't sorry. The very idea of her here, *alone*, chilled his blood.

He wiped a hand over his face, his head, worked at the kinks in his neck. With a long look at her closed bedroom door, he stood and stretched. He'd grabbed his computer bag, toiletries and a change of clothes last night, after she'd locked herself in her bedroom, but with her in the shower now, he could brace both doors open as he'd done last night, grab his suitcase and be back before she turned off the water.

Decision made, he headed for the door and pulled it open.

The room service cart from dinner was gone. He'd heard it being rolled away somewhere around ten. Then there had been nothing except the storm, which had raged a few times during the night. He glanced over his shoulder, at Calea's bedroom door.

Water still gurgled so he turned back and stepped into the hall. Pressure lifted and he could breathe easily again.

On an inward breath of air, he reached for the doorknob of his hotel room.

His fingers barely touching the metal, a faint sense of agitation sparked against his fingertips. He yanked his hand back.

What the hell?

He turned his hand over to stare at his fingertips, rubbed them together.

But the sensations didn't go away.

Pissed. Frustrated.

Not his own feelings. Simply impressions. Low level, but there.

He held his fingers less than an inch from the doorknob. Nothing. He lowered his hand, closer. There. At about a quarter inch from the surface. Faint. But there.

Son of a bitch.

Hoffman had been in his room sometime during the night.

When the man had rolled the service cart away? Had he taken a few extra moments to search Gavin's room?

Hoffman would have had to have been quick. And quiet about it.

Why hadn't he or Calea heard or *felt* something?

The man needed to be taught a few lessons.

Gavin ran a hand over the top of his head. His cheek twitched.

Another time, perhaps.

This morning, his priority was getting Calea away from here, to the airport and safely ensconced back at the Institute.

Where he knew he didn't have to worry about her safety.

He gripped the doorknob, slid his room card in and out of the slot then shoved the door open.

Absolute chaos.

His gut tightened. His hands fisted.

Son of a freaking bitch.

Covers, yanked off the bed, tangled with bath towels in a heap in the center of the room. Broken glass lay strewn across the floor. Even the drapes were torn from the windows.

Thankful he'd collected a few things the night before, he stood, legs spread and hands on hips, to survey the damage.

Chaos might not be the word to cover this destruction.

His black suitcase, one of his favorites, lay on the floor, across the room from where he'd left it, upside down with knife slashes torn through the tough exterior material. His clothing had met the same fate.

Hoffman was one angry man.

Gavin's mouth tightened. Why the hell hadn't he heard any of this last night, while it was happening? How the hell had Roy kept this manic demolition contained? Off the psychic radar? Why hadn't Gavin, or at the very least Calea, who was much better at this stuff, sensed this was going on?

Last night, Gavin would have sworn the man was a null. No abilities. No shielding. Nothing. Nada.

Hoffman had appeared to be an opportunist, making decisions on the fly.

Disorganized.

Chaos itself as a shield? As a barrier?

Shit.

He'd underestimated the bartender. What other conclusion could there be?

Gavin glanced back through his open door into Calea's room across the hallway.

What the hell did Hoffman want with her?

And if the man *could* block Gavin from tapping into his intentions, then how the hell was Gavin going to protect her? Keep her from harm?

Keep her alive?

Chapter Four

CALEA WRINKLED HER nose at her reflection in the bathroom mirror. Uneasiness that wasn't hers skittered over her skin.

Gavin's?

She angled her head, stretched her senses a little farther. Her shields hadn't been breached, but he wasn't in the other room. He'd gone across the hall.

Anger pulsed underneath the edginess.

She blinked twice. Definitely Gavin. Not in any physical harm. No one else with him.

But he was furious.

Did she want to head over there, find out what had him so agitated?

Not really. She'd given one Gavin Dunbar way too much of her time, her thoughts, her soul. Just too much.

And now she was going to let him take her back to the Institute to where he could lock her back away, to where he didn't have to worry about her.

Where it was easier for him to put her on the back burner and just pop in once in a while to make sure she was still around. Still there.

Like a damn touchstone.

Damn him.

If he wasn't completely accurate about the danger, she'd enjoy giving him the slip. Enjoy sticking his bossiness and arrogance right up his ass.

But she didn't want to die.

And while that glimmer she'd seen, the one that indicated there might be someone else for him and that, *lucky her*, she might, one day soon, actually *see* the face of whoever that new woman might be, could mean her time was nearer than she thought, she had no intentions of going easy.

Which meant it was time to leave here. Get out of Oregon. To swallow her damn pride and accept Gavin's help.

For now.

Her touch light, she slid her fingertips down the braid she'd pulled to one side, so that it lay over her right shoulder. The pink ribbon she'd threaded through was a few shades lighter than the rose sweater she'd paired with her black jeans. She looked good. Not that it mattered.

Gavin had sworn off her. Off their relationship. Off any kind of future together.

No matter that the attraction between them was as white hot as it'd ever been.

As strong and volatile as the storm that had raged through last night.

But while that storm seemed to have passed, unlike the one in her heart, another was predicted to swoop in later this morning. Within the next two hours.

If they were going to make it to the small airport and out of the area before the weather turned bad again, they should probably get on the road.

On a deep breath, braced and ready, she raised her chin and swung her bedroom door open. All she had to do was get through this day with as much dignity as possible. Head back to the Institute, have a long talk with Ben. Figure out her next steps.

Move on without Gavin.

Her throat tightened and her heart stuttered.

She had to. Being stuck in limbo was killing her.

As she's suspected, her front door was wide open so she moved towards it, grabbing her long, black flashlight along the way. She hadn't *felt* any danger to Gavin, but being prepared was always better and she knew how to use the light as a weapon.

Across the hallway, Gavin stood in the open doorway of his own room.

Relief welled and spilled over inside her.

Stupid. She *knew* he was okay. But *seeing* him okay released a damn torrent of emotion, choking her. She could barely swallow. "Gavin?"

He turned his head to look at her over his shoulder. Sunlight streamed into his room, haloing him in a golden glow. His eyes, though, she saw clearly and pissed off didn't even begin to describe the anger flaring in those storm-tossed depths.

That stupid relief mixed with dread.

"What?" She tried to look around him, but between the bright light and his big body, most of her view was blocked.

His cell phone in one hand, he stepped backwards and pulled the door closed before he turned to face her. "Hoffman. He's a bigger problem than I realized."

Self-disgust laced Gavin's voice. He glanced down the hall in both directions before shooing her back in to her room and shutting then latching the security locks on her door.

"Gavin?" She leaned against the wall as he strode to the center of her room. "What happened? What did Roy do to your room?"

"Destroyed it."

All the air left her lungs. She bent forward, as if an invisible fist had landed in her stomach. "Why?"

"At a guess, I'd say he's seriously pissed." He motioned her to one of the wing-backed chairs while he paced the room. "At me."

The sudden ring of his phone sent tremors across her skin.

"Dunbar." With his cell to his ear and his mouth set in a tight line, Gavin stopped near the edge of the bank of windows, at an angle to her, and braced one hand flat on the wall while he stared out at the Pacific Ocean.

She sat in one of the wing-backed chairs and braced her bare feet on the edge then wrapped her arms around her knees. Why hadn't she *felt* whatever the hell it was Roy had done in Gavin's room? The disturbance, the anger, should have, at the least, brushed against her shields.

Alerted her.

She shivered.

"That data I asked for last night, where is it?" Gavin's eyes narrowed as he spoke into his phone.

So cold. She ran her palms over the sleeves of her sweater.

"The bartender, Roy Hoffman?" Gavin's voice hardened. "What's the rest of his story?"

Who the hell is Roy? That Gavin couldn't *read* him and she hadn't *felt* his destructive acts just across the hallway?

"ASAP." Gavin snapped off the word then hung up. With the pad of his thumb he scrolled across the screen to press another number before he again held the cell to his ear. "Ben, Gavin. I need anything you have, anything you can find on Roy Hoffman. Bartender here."

He listened for a moment. Spared her a glance then again focused on the view outside her windows.

"Latent psychic ability of some kind. Possibly a blocker." He listened for a moment. Shook his head. "Last night I might have said a null. Today, no way in hell."

Calea angled her head to rest her cheek on her knees and stare out at the Pacific, keeping Gavin in her peripheral vision, while he gave Ben an abbreviated version of the events of the last fifteen hours.

"The bastard blocked me. Blocked Calea. Like he's hiding in plain sight." Gavin's voice washed over her. "I have someone on it from my side. I'll have his past under a microscope. But what I want, what I need, is the guy's psychic profile. If he has one."

Her shivers chased themselves over her skin.

"You'll have what I have as soon as I have it." Gavin thumbed the off switch of his cell, holstered it and set both hands on his hips. He continued to stare out at the water. "I'm correct in my assumption, aren't I? That you felt nothing from the direction of my room during the night?"

"Do you really need to ask that?"

"No." He twisted his head from side to side.

Her fingers itched to rub his shoulders, to help relieve the tension locked there. Instead, she curled her fingers into fists and tightened her arms around her legs. "Then why did you?"

His head back, he closed his eyes for a long moment. "No idea."

Right.

"You're packed and I have nothing to pack. I'll get cleaned up and we're out of here."

On a nod, she stretched, stood and headed for the bedroom for her shoes and her luggage. Behind her, Gavin's cell dinged, a sound she knew indicated incoming messages.

Roy Hoffman's life in a nutshell.

At least the surface of it. Once Ben's people got through with the data and whatever else they could dig up, they'd know a whole lot more about what made the bartender tick.

And why.

That part scared her.

The *why* of what he'd done.

GAVIN, HIS COMPUTER bag slung over his shoulder and pulling Calea's rolling suitcase, strode across the lobby towards the exit for the parking structure with Calea right next to him.

Past time to blow this place.

"Mr. Dunbar?" John, the hotel manager, hurried towards them.

Impatient, Gavin stopped and turned toward the tall, lean man. They'd talked earlier, when Gavin had called down to report the vandalism.

"Once again, Mr. Dunbar, our deepest apologies for what happened to your room. The authorities have been called –" He glanced between them. "But they can't get in and I'm afraid you won't be able to leave just yet."

"Excuse me?"

John swallowed, his throat working. "The road is out."

"How?"

The man swallowed again. "We're not sure. Possibly – probably – from the storm. The Sheriff's deputy who called a few minutes ago didn't say. He only would confirm we're all kind of stuck here for the time being."

"Like hell." Gavin pulled his cell from its holder at his hip and dialed Mac, the pilot of the plane that had brought him here. There'd been a helicopter tucked into a private hanger at the small airport. And since Mac could fly anything, problem solved.

"No go." The connection bad, Mac's rusty voice echoed in his ear. "—stolen less than an half an hour ago."

"What was stolen?"

"Between —" Static mixed and muffled half the pilot's words. "Told we can't leave yet."

The line went dead.

Gavin's phone beeped. No service.

Shit.

The road was out. Something, maybe the helicopter, had been stolen a half hour ago.

Gavin didn't believe in coincidences.

He believed in being prepared.

"Your phone?" He sent Calea a sideways look.

She slid hers from her front pocket, checked it and, her own gaze troubled, met his and shook her head. "Nothing."

He turned to the manager. "Where is Hoffman?"

"I'm not sure." The man shrugged. "His shift ended at midnight."

"Where does he live? The other side of the road that's out? Or on this side?"

"This side." John glanced between him and Calea. "He's staying at his aunt's place, near the edge of the hotel property. But he's not answering my calls so I don't know if he's there or not."

Which could mean many different things. "How many guests do you have?"

"This is off-season and we've had a usually high number of cancellations this last week due to renovations and the series of storms battering the coast."

"How many guests?"

John swallowed again. "Just the two of you."

"Staff?"

"Also two. My chef and myself. We both live on the premises. The other two scheduled for this morning live on the other side of the road closure and can't make it in. Roy isn't due back until late afternoon."

Gavin scanned the lobby. So four people, including himself and Calea. Five if Hoffman happened to be lurking around. "And the Sheriff's Department didn't give you any clue about how long the road would be out?"

"No."

"Does this happen often?"

John, a frown marring his forehead, shook his head. "I don't remember it ever happening."

Prickles inched their way up Gavin's spine. No coincidences.

"But the deputy said he'd call as soon as the road is open." John spread his hands.

So maybe they didn't think it would be that long. "I need a phone that works."

"On the concierge level we have a full office, phones, computers, faxes." John waved a hand towards the counter. "Let me store your luggage until you're able to leave. And have the chef bring you breakfast while you wait."

"Thank you." Calea's smile, calm and gracious, had the man hurrying forward to take the case from Gavin.

Thirty minutes later it was obvious they weren't going to be able to connect with the outside world. All phone lines, land and cell, were now down.

Son of a bitch.

Gavin paced from one side of the spacious room to the other. Calea, sitting on the couch against the far wall, watched him. He ran a hand over his mouth and jaw, along the stubble he hadn't taken the time to shave earlier.

"Did you read anything negative off of John?"

"No." He moved to the window. Similar view to Calea's, only from the top floor.

"Stop doubting yourself, Gavin."

He frowned, but kept his gaze on the turbulent waves rolling in towards the cliffs.

She'd always been too perceptive. Always saw more than he wanted her to see.

"If Roy is a natural blocker, there's nothing you could have done to read him."

Right. And how the hell was he going to protect her if he didn't know what direction the danger was coming from?

"Gavin?" She half rose from her seat.

He held up a hand, palm towards her. "This whole thing seems off. Wrong."

She settled back, pulled a small pillow onto to her lap. "More than Roy Hoffman?"

"Yeah. The road being out. The helicopter stolen." He pressed a hand to the wall beside the window.

"Are you feeling that way because we're isolated? Cut off?"

One side of his mouth lifted. She was dangerous. A psychic with a psychology degree who also *actually* understood people. "Maybe."

And that was him. Non-committal. "Or maybe because there's a threat I can't figure out. Can't pinpoint the direction."

Now it was her turn to frown. "Is this something new for you? *Feeling* something in the ether that isn't connected to someone you're actually reading?"

Dangerous ground. Ground he didn't intend to cover, not with her.

He waved the hand not braced against the wall. "Stop psycho analyzing me, Calea."

"Hmmm."

"Like you, I'm not some super-psychic agent and if it bothers me that I can't read someone I think I should be able to read, there's nothing *hmmm* about it."

She raised one of those perfect eyebrows but didn't say a word.

Dammit all.

He *knew* the routine. Knew the psyche games.

Fell for hers every single damn time.

"I don't like being blind." He fisted the hand against the wall. "I don't like *knowing* there's something off and not being able to pinpoint it. To pinpoint the threat."

"That's just being human, Gavin."

"Doesn't help when everything that's happening doesn't add up."

"There are people out there you can't read. Natural blockers, or maybe, with Roy, it's a learned behavior. We don't know, might never know, even after your report comes in."

He'd sent what little his resources had gathered earlier immediately to Ben, but it wasn't much. Roy Hoffman seemed to be off the grid as far as he could tell. If that was even the man's real name. "All right. What's your take, then? Is Hoffman a natural?"

Her gaze on him, she settled back against the couch.

"If not, if it's learned, why?" His words clipped, he faced her with his legs apart and his hands fisted on his hips. "What would it take to manifest that skill?"

"The need to stay under the radar of an abuser."

"Really?"

"It's a possibility."

"How about the *desire* to stay under the radar? To do whatever the hell it is you want without getting caught? To manipulate the system for your own gain?"

She frowned.

"Sometimes people are just bad, Calea. No redeeming qualities."

"You asked –"

"And *understanding* them, seeing them as a victim, only muddies the waters."

"Gavin –"

"I'm not going to stand by and let you be victimized because of a soft heart."

"You aren't responsible for me, dammit. Or my soft heart."

"So I'm supposed to stand by and let someone obsess over you? Hurt you?"

"That's not at all what I said. You're twisting things, Gavin."

"Maybe I am. And maybe you need to get over it. I *refuse* to let that son of a bitch get to you like my father did my mother. You will not die on my watch."

Chapter Five

CALEA LEANED BACK against the couch in the concierge and hugged a throw pillow close to her chest.

You will not die on my watch.

I refuse to let that son of a bitch get to you ... like my father did to my mother.

Oh Lord, Gavin.

The pain radiating from him filled her, all the nooks and crannies in her heart, her soul.

This was new, a crack opening an interior he kept completely closed off.

That was at the root of everything for Gavin.

His mother's death.

Was he implying his father had killed her? Or that his father had taken advantage of the woman's empathic abilities and had somehow been responsible for her death?

"Was that when your own abilities manifested? When your mother died?"

His hands in fists at his sides, he turned away from her. Shut down.

"Gavin –"

"None of that matters."

Oh yes, it mattered. A helluva lot, it mattered. And answered as many questions as it posed.

"I'm not asking you to stand by and let me be hurt."

"Aren't you?" He angled his head toward her, his eyes filled with dark clouds. "Isn't that *exactly* what you're asking of me?"

What the hell was she asking of him?

To love me.

No. Those days were over. She shook the thoughts aside. "You're twisting things. Making them fit to justify your actions."

He turned fully towards her, those dark clouds in his eyes a full blown storm.

Guess that got a reaction.

She lifted her chin.

"Why is it so wrong to want to protect you? Keep you safe?"

"I'm not yours to protect. Not any longer."

His eyes narrowed, but like hell she was backing down.

After several drawn out seconds he wiped a hand over his mouth. "Maybe you're not. But that doesn't lessen your importance. To the Institute. To Ben. To the PSI. Even if I could leave here without you, I'm not going to. Don't ask that of me."

She closed her eyes. Closed out the sight of him.

What had she expected? To be important to *him*?

On a sigh, she opened her eyes, ran a hand over the top of her head, down her braid to fiddle with the ends of the ribbon. "I'm not asking that."

"Then why are we fighting?"

"Is that what we're doing?"

"Calea, there's no easy answer to what's between us now. We need to simply focus on getting through this current threat." He turned back to the window. "Get you back to the Institute."

Where he could dump her and run.

She knew how this worked.

He didn't want her, but the thought of her out in the world without him totally freaked him out. Keep her safe, behind the Institute's walls. Away from threat. Away from danger. Away from ….

Strike that.

She tilted her head to study his profile and the way a sudden ray of sunshine, bursting from behind the clouds and glinting though the glass, encased him in its light.

He *did* want her. Had always wanted her. From the beginning the chemistry between them had been hot. Instant.

Had threatened to consume them both.

That's what freaked him the most.

More than anything?

Was it *simply* that he couldn't cope with being out of control?

No.

Although he was a control freak, to put it mildly, it had to be more than that.

Back to his mother's death?

He'd sidestepped that conversation.

Had they ever talked about his mother? About her death?

He'd been young, barely a teenager, if she remembered correctly.

"Gavin –"

"Where's that chef with our breakfast?"

Change of subject.

Maybe he was right. Maybe she needed time to absorb these latest insights, to find out more about his mother's death and then grill Ben about the entire episode. The smart thing would be to focus on the now of it all, to have breakfast, wait for the road to be cleared and stay away from Roy Hoffman.

Smart and sane, that was her motto in life. Except where Gavin was concerned. Only now, that had to be her new mantra with him. Smart and sane and keep her heart locked away. Protected.

"You're quiet." His soft voice brought her head up.

Her lips twitched at the suspicion lurking in his eyes. "I'm just thinking."

"And?"

"Wondering where that chef is with our breakfast."

Two could play that game.

He stared at her for several heartbeats, looked like he might say something then shook his head. "I'll call down and find out."

From under her lashes she watched him stride across the room to the phone, watched him dial, wait and then hang-up to redial. After several attempts, he looked at her over his shoulder. "No one is picking up. Not at the front desk. John's office or the kitchen."

"Maybe they're both busy."

"Doing what? We're the only guests."

"I don't know. Hotel stuff."

"Feels wrong." Hand on his hips, a deep frown marred his forehead. "You're not getting anything?"

No." But then she'd been preoccupied, even knowing she needed to concentrate on her surroundings, she'd let her thoughts wander. Enough of that. She tilted her head, let her gaze go soft and unfocused. Stretched out her senses.

No real disturbances, not on the surface.

She explored further. Wider. Deeper.

Nothing tangible. Nothing to lock on to.

A niggle of … what was that?

Fear?

She teased the impression, stroked the fiber of it.

Followed the thread down its length.

Banged up against a slammed door.

An acrid, burnt smell filled her nose. Pain radiated from her left shoulder down her arm to spasm through to her fingertips.

What –? Her breathing quickened. Her lungs burned. Her vision shifted from soft to muddy.

She shook her head. Focused on the blurred outline of her hands, on her twitching fingers she'd laced together over the small pillow. Blinking several times, she struggled to sharpen her vision.

"What the hell just happened?" Gavin knelt in front of her. His hands gripped her upper arms. Anchored her. Warmth seeped into her skin from his touch and her breathing slowed. The muddiness swirled and began to fade a slight bit.

She concentrated on his eyes. On his gaze. On the life support she found there.

"Calea? Sweetheart. Answer me."

"Ga ... vin."

"You're trembling."

Panic filled her as he straightened. "Don't ... leave ... me."

"I'm not going anywhere without you." He sat on the couch next to her, pulled her onto his lap and cradled her against his chest, tight in his arms. "It's okay, sweetheart."

She burrowed into his warmth, pressed her face to his neck. Inhaled the spicy, masculine scent of him, let that obliterate the burnt stench clinging to her insides.

"Where were you?" His voice soft against her hair, he pressed his lips to her temple.

Not sure how to answer, not sure she knew the answer, she shook her head.

"What did you pick up?"

"At first, there was nothing. As if you and I were the only ones in this building. Completely alone." Her shields shaky but in place, she burrowed closer as she went back over it in her mind. "Then there was a thin, almost negligible, spurt of fear."

Gavin's arms tightened a fraction.

"Nothing tangible to the feeling, it certainly wasn't strong. It didn't pulse or flare. More of an undercurrent."

"You followed it?" The slightest hint of stress lined his voice.

She nodded into his neck. "It wavered just a bit when I stroked it but then settled."

"And then?"

"Something slammed into me. Like a steel door." Her voice trembled. "And then you called my name."

"You were gone a solid five minutes, Calea."

"It only felt like a few moments." She pulled back, immediately missed his warmth. Grateful for the arms still around her, she met his troubled gaze.

"You were in control the whole time?"

"Yes." She paused. "I don't know. I thought I was, but I'd swear I wasn't gone that long."

"I timed it. When you started to sway and blink your eyes, but not into focus, you'd been gone long enough."

"Thank you." She ran the tips of her fingers along his cheek then pressed her lips to his jaw. "For being here. For anchoring me."

Even when she hadn't realized she needed anchoring.

With a slight turn of his head, he captured her mouth with his, suckled her bottom lip.

Heat swelled inside her, melted her at her core.

Oh, God.

Her tongue met his, tangled.

In his arms, she pressed against him, her breasts heavy and full of ache.

For him. For his touch.

"Gavin." She breathed his name. Breathed him.

His hands ran down her back, pressed her closer.

Heat burst through to ignite every nerve ending. Her breath caught in her throat, held.

Home. This was where she was supposed to be. With him. In his arms.

Gavin.

He groaned against her mouth.

A tremor of a different type thudded through her blood, pounded in her ears.

"This is insane." His words whispered through her. Chilled her.

She turned her head, his lips brushed her cheek and sent tingles cascading across her skin.

"We need to stop." His forehead rested against hers.

She pressed her eyelids tight. "Why? Because there's no future in *this*?"

"Calea."

She pulled away from him, held up a hand. "For a man who denies the future has any hold over him, you sure exhibit a marked fear of it."

His eyes narrowed, he dropped his hands from her back, letting her push herself off his lap while he leaned back against the couch.

She stood, her legs trembling, and with her arms crossed over her chest, stared down at him. He met her gaze, glare for glare, until she shook her head and spun away from him.

He was right. This was insane. And she was insane to care so damn much.

"What next?" She tossed the words over her shoulder. "Maybe John and his chef are outside. When I scanned the area, it felt as if you and I were the only ones in the building."

Silence prevailed for long seconds but she would be damned before she would look at him right now.

"What about whatever the hell that was that slammed into you?" Controlled anger edged his voice.

She lifted her chin, stared at the darkening clouds hovering over the ocean outside the windows. "I have no idea whose fear I tapped into."

He sighed, deep with fake patience designed to piss her off. She set her jaw.

"Whoever it belonged to, do you think that's who slammed the door on your connection?"

She frowned at the window. Had that *someone* actually felt her? Actually severed the link she'd forged to that tenuous thread of emotion? To her knowledge, Gavin was the only one who'd been able to *feel* her in that way.

One arm around her waist, she pressed a hand to the collar of her sweater at the base of her throat. "I guess that's possible. But it didn't seem the same. Different intensity. Different core. Just different."

"Okay, then." A *different* kind of tension coated his voice. Her answer bothered him.

Bothered her, too.

"Calea, am I wrong in thinking there's an issue here? Of someone being able to *sense* you when you're locked into someone else? Do you see that the way I am?"

Oh she saw it and it made her tremble.

Literally.

"You're not wrong." She pulled the edge of her collar away from her neck. "I'm just not sure what to do about it. If there is anything to do about it. Beyond keep my shields in place."

"I'm not sure that's a deterrent."

Me, either. "It's all I have right now."

"You have me."

At the quietness of his voice, she angled her head to glance at him over her shoulder. His grey eyes, dark with emotion, held hers.

She had him.

Until he could deposit her back at the Institute.

Then she'd be *alone* once again.

Chapter Six

GAVIN SQUEEZED CALEA'S fingers, laced them through his and gave her what he hoped was a reassuring smile. They stood in the hallway, in front of the elevator bank, of the hotel's top floor, several feet from the concierge room, their computer bags slung over their shoulders.

Mid-morning. No breakfast. No one answering their calls to the front desk or the hotel office. Not even the kitchen. The hotel *felt* empty. Abandoned. No outside phone service. No internet service. Not even the damned television in the concierge would come in.

They were well and truly cut off from the outside.

Bad weather aside, the question was why.

And, really, who.

Roy, the klutz, Hoffman?

Could the man pull this, whatever this was, off? All on his own?

Why?

Seemed over the top.

Were they being paranoid?

Probably.

That had kept Gavin alive more than once.

That next storm had yet to make landfall. He wanted them out of this place, down that road as far as it would take them before the rain started again. They could regroup at that point.

Because here, right now, in this hotel, his neck itched.

Like they had huge red targets painted on their backs.

Good enough reason to get the hell out.

Never mind that damn kiss he shouldn't have taken, couldn't wipe from his mind.

Calea Fontaine was well and truly under his skin, no matter what the hell he told himself.

Another damn good reason to get out of here. Before he did something *really* stupid.

He scanned the white numbers above each elevator door, the numbers indicating which floor a particular elevator was on. Three of the four read L for Lobby. The last was on the seventh floor.

Their rooms were on that floor.

Coincidence?

Doubtful.

The light changed to number eight.

Whoever was in that elevator was heading upwards.

He tugged on her hand. "Stairs."

She glanced at the blinking number then, with her finger still laced with his, followed him into the stairwell. There he eased the door closed behind them.

"Where to?" Her words, whispered, hung between them.

He had no clue.

For all they knew the chef was finally bringing them breakfast.

Not that Gavin believed that.

Hanging around to find out didn't seem like a viable option.

"Down." From behind the door he heard the ding of the elevator. He held his index finger to his lips and mouthed the word *wait*.

She nodded and tilted her head to the side.

Shit. She wasn't reaching out was she? They didn't know –

He squeezed her fingers.

You think I'm insane? The annoyance in her shadow filled gaze said it all.

No.

Not insane.

Just not sure he trusted her caution.

Had she ever really been in a situation quite like this one?

When Milford's goons had gone after her, it had all been so quick. Without warning.

And her training had kicked in.

He needed to remember that. Give her the credit she deserved.

Trust her instincts.

Damn hard to do that when all he wanted was to keep her safe.

A light shimmer touched him, enveloped him. Pressed against his skin. Squeezed his lungs.

He swallowed once. Rotated his shoulders.

Calea's shields. Stretched to encompass him.

Maybe he should've known that's what she would do. Maybe. Considering he wasn't any good at shielding, it wasn't the first thing he reached for, wasn't his first choice. Then there was the claustrophobic factor.

And maybe her shields weren't too late, maybe whoever that was out there hadn't already *felt* them.

Maybe.

He swallowed again.

Maintain. Focus. Ignore the pressure bearing down on him from the shields.

Get through the crisis. Breathe again.

The elevator door whooshed to close followed by a soft metallic click.

The elevator? Or something else?

He let go of her hand to shift the weight of his computer bag then he pulled his gun from where he'd stashed it at the small of his back, held it against his leg, his trigger finger straight along the barrel.

Footsteps, quiet and no more than a soft slide against thick carpet, echoed from the area in front of the elevator to just the other side of the stairwell door.

The steps paused.

Calea's breath held, her shield in place.

The door handle moved a fraction.

Gavin lifted his arms, cupped the butt of his weapon and moved his index finger to hover over the trigger.

The handle eased back into position and those soft footfalls slid away, as quietly as before, until one of the doors on the other side of the elevator bank, leading into the concierge, opened then closed.

Calea raised an eyebrow.

Gavin shook his head one time.

His neck still itched.

It wasn't time to move.

Not yet.

After what felt like an eternity, a low masculine curse stretched through the door.

Gavin's stomach muscles tightened.

He'd half expected this, bait and switch, wasn't surprised.

But it changed the field.

Considerably.

The concierge door opened again. This time it didn't swing closed. Whoever was out there probably had it open and even now stood scoping out the empty room.

Gavin checked his watch. Fifteen minutes since he'd last tried to reach the front desk from the phone in that room. Fifteen minutes that meant he and Calea couldn't have gone far.

And all the elevators, except one, were on the lobby level.

That left the stairs.

Whoever that was on the other side of the door would be in here in short order.

Gavin glanced behind him, at the stairs.

Metal.

That would echo as soon as they stepped down.

But what choice did they have?

He caught Calea's gaze, again put his index finger to his lips. She nodded.

Keep the shield in place. He twirled his finger in a circle.

She nodded again.

All right then.

Shit.

He kept his arms up, elbows bent with his trigger finger again along the barrel.

Time to move.

Backwards. Facing the door, the threat.

His body angled so he could see both Calea and the door, he motioned to her to take that first, freaking step.

She gripped the strap of her computer bag at her left shoulder, her arm against the outside of the case to keep it in place. Facing forward, she eased one foot backwards and down a step.

Paused. They both listened.

Nothing.

He nodded once then she eased her other foot down.

Tension ratcheted, pressed against the confines of Calea's shield, against his too tight skin. *That* he could feel.

That was why he didn't do the shield thing.

Fed his claustrophobia.

He swallowed against the hard knot in his throat. No choice. *Get through this.*

Sideways, he took his own step down. Then another.

A slight squeak.

Calea's eyes widened. She pressed her lips together.

He jerked his head once, then gave a short, two fingered double wave over the barrel of his gun. *Keep going, sweetheart.* One step at a time.

He rotated his head, lifted his chin. If anyone came through that door, he'd take care of it.

After several terse moments of slow movements, they stepped onto the landing. Half a floor down. Minimum of another half to go.

If they got out on the ninth floor.

They had *to get out on the ninth floor.*

He *needed* these damn shields wider. Less confining. Less against his skin. Cutting off his breath. Choking him.

A light line of sweat beaded across his forehead.

Shit.

"Little faster." Although the words vibrated in his chest, he knew he'd only whispered them. He couldn't hear past the pounding thud of his own heart.

Her hand touched his back, a small spark of heat, there then gone, then she was several steps down from him, waiting at the ninth floor landing.

Once there, with his gun up and leading, he eased open the door and scanned the hallway opening to the elevator bank. Nothing. No one in front or in either direction. Each number over each elevator was exactly the same as before.

So whoever had decided to join them in the concierge room was still up there.

He slipped out of the stairwell, eased the door closed after Calea.

Immediately her shields expanded, fit the contours of the hallway.

Sound exploded in his ears.

Her shallow breaths, the soft click of the stairwell door.

The clang of ice dropping in an ice machine.

His own breath as he pulled air into his burning lungs.

"Gavin." Calea's soft voice echoed through him.

He turned to her. She held up a key. He frowned.

That was the concierge key John had given her.

"I think this is a master room key and will work on any of the rooms."

"We need to find another set of stairs. Get to my vehicle." And damned if he knew if there even was *another* set of stairs. "Not get into another room."

"And there's a map of the building on the back of every room door."

Damned if she wasn't right.

He nodded and pulled at his collar. "Pick a room, sweetheart."

With a quick nod, she stepped to the left, to the door opposite the elevator and at an angle to the stairwell.

Excellent choice.

She slid in the key, twisted the knob and the door swung open. With a quick glance over her shoulder, her eyes bright with victory, she slipped inside. He was right behind her and had the door closed and the deadbolt latched then stood, legs shoulder width apart, knees locked, with his gun held down by his leg. His head back, he sucked in several deep gulps of air.

"Gavin?" Concern laced her low voice.

"Widen those shields of yours. More." He held up his free hand, palm forward. "Please."

In less than a fraction of a second the constricted bands of pressure around his chest eased to just bearable. He spared a quick glance around the room. A suite, similar to Calea's, with a wide bank of windows on the opposite wall. Heavy drapes bracketed the glass, exposing a grey, angry ocean, tossed by incoming winds.

The storm was going to be harsh.

"What's going on with you?" Calea touched his arm. That quick spark of heat flitted across his skin.

He shook his head, moved away from her to the door. "Not important. I'm fine, now. We need to find that other way out here."

Her eyes full of doubt, she joined him, without touching, to study the hotel diagram on the back of the door. There was another set of stairs going from the parking structure below the bottom floor to the kitchen area of the concierge room. In addition, there was also a single service elevator close to those stairs.

Getting to either of those might be dicey.

"You believe that was Roy in the elevator." She didn't look at him, just pressed her eye to the spyhole. "How do we make sure?"

"Lure him out without giving away our position."

"Right." Derision coated the one word. "Easy as cake."

"I press down to call the elevator. Once it gets here, I press the lobby button, duck in here with you and we wait to see who shows up." He shrugged.

Who said cake was hard?

"So you want to make it look like we *were* on this floor, but then went to the lobby?"

"Yep."

"And if he's already in the lobby to greet an empty elevator?"

"Then we stay really quiet when he comes up here to check on us."

She angled her head to stare at him a moment. Then she shrugged. "Why not?"

"Stay here." He gripped the door handle.

Her touch light, she stroked two fingers along the back of his hand. "I can't take the shields down all the way, Gavin."

"I didn't ask you to."

"But I'll try to keep them wide."

"Do what you need to do." And he'd pray he'd be able to maintain. He pulled open the door, took the few steps across the hall and hit the down arrow then counted the seconds for the elevator to descend from the tenth floor.

He stood with his legs shoulder width apart, both hands braced on the butt of his weapon and his gaze sighted down the barrel.

The elevator settled. Dinged once and the doors slid open.

Empty.

Perfect. He reached in, hit the lobby button and was back in the room with Calea before the doors closed.

He stood with the hotel door open less than inch and scanned the hallway while she had her eye pressed to the spyhole. This would work as long as Hoffman didn't head down the kitchen elevator or take the –

A thud sounded on the other side of the nearest wall. Stairs.

Calea, her eyes dark, glanced at him then backed up. Her shields locked down, but not on top of him. More like they settled into the walls of the room.

He could still breathe. For now.

He eased the door shut and with his weapon between him and the door, he took her place at the spyhole. Out of caution, training, he widened his stance, so that anyone looking wouldn't see a shadow under the door. One that didn't belong.

The door to the stairwell opened. The tip of a gun barrel poked out.

So much for this being simple paranoia.

Roy Hoffman moved, slow and with stealth, into the hallway, his gun following his head as he scanned the area. His other hand behind him, he braced the stairwell door until it simply clicked closed.

So Roy didn't want anyone knowing he was here, either.

The klutz seemed to have disappeared.

If he ever actually existed.

The man's gaze swept the hallway, then lower, checking the floor along the rooms opposite them.

Looking for those shadows that didn't belong.

Even without Gavin's stance, they should be fine. No lights on in the room. Any morning sunshine that happened to push through the clouds would be on the other side of the building. And the heavy storm clouds kept this room dark.

But Roy checked.

Training.

Who the hell was this guy?

The man's gaze went to the elevator, to the numbers above the elevator. The tense line of his shoulders eased a fraction. He nodded once, but still turned towards the hallway. Towards their door.

Narrowed eyes, dark brown with flecks of green and gold, as flat and deadly as any Gavin had ever seen, stared directly at their door.

Gavin had his answer about *who* hunted them.

A bad dude with a bad agenda.

Chapter Seven

C ALEA STOOD STONE still.

Whatever, whoever, was on the other side of their borrowed, closed, hotel door, was probing in ways she'd never been subjected to, never experienced.

Her breathing shallow, she continued, with each out breath, to project *emptiness* into her shields, fought against an intense desire to wrap those same shields tight around both her and Gavin.

She couldn't do that.

Mostly because the shift would give away their presence, but also because Gavin couldn't operate with her shields that close. She'd seen that firsthand, in the stairwell, not more than a few minutes ago.

Although right now it felt more like years than minutes.

She'd hold on. What choice did she have?

The probe changed. Eased back. The tendrils flowing away.

But Gavin's posture didn't change.

Being an agent hadn't been for her, but she remembered the lessons. And the reasons for the lessons. Then there was that kidnap attempt all those months ago. Determined to sidestep any possible traps, she'd take her cues from Gavin and continue on until he told her different.

Shallow breath in. shallow breath out.

Emptiness.

A sudden thud sounded again, from behind the wall next to her. Several metallic thumps echoed through the room.

Her heart stuttered.

Shallow breath in.

Someone was in the stairwell, heading downward if she heard the noise correctly.

Gavin continued to keep his eye pressed to the spyhole.

Shallow breath out.

Emptiness.

"All clear." His low voice brushed over her.

She sucked in a deep breath. Pressed her hands to her face.

"It was Roy Hoffman."

Her stomach tightened.

She'd known Gavin had thought it was Roy, she'd hoped he was wrong. Had hoped it was all paranoia on their part.

"Why?"

Gavin shook his head.

"What next?"

"Different room."

"But he left down the stairwell." Her hands pressed to her cheeks, she spun towards him. "Didn't he? I heard him. If he knew we were here –"

"He left." Gavin checked his weapon. "I'm just not sure he won't be back."

"Why would he be?"

"Because he sensed *something*. He just isn't sure what that something is. When he doesn't find us in the lobby I have a suspicion he'll be back here."

"He's a hunter, isn't he?"

Gavin grimaced and rotated his head before he met her gaze. "If he's not, he should be."

A NEW FLOOR, a new room.

Calea tapped her fingers around the bottle of sparkling water she held and pressed her head back against the wing-backed chair she sat on in front of the windows overlooking the water.

Several hours had passed since she and Gavin had hurried to the service set of stairs, headed back up to the tenth floor and entered the presidential suite down the hall from the concierge room. In here, the drapes were pulled back to reveal those lowering clouds as the storm pushed in from the ocean and the sun hid behind those ominous clouds.

Since they'd been in here, she'd helped Gavin take closet rods out and wedge them across both exit doors in makeshift locks. They'd also shoved a chair under the doorknob of the door on their side that separated this suite from the one next door.

All that in addition to the deadbolts on all doors.

Just in case Roy did find them and thought to come in here from that direction.

Her shields were in place, fortified and settled into to the walls of the room, with an early detection option, as she liked to think of it, attached. Something that took some doing on her part, something she couldn't do on the fly. But something she'd finessed in the last few hours.

After having had a taste of Roy's probe, she was fairly sure she'd feel it if he came close again. If he even stepped onto this floor.

Now, as lightning flashed over the ocean, she sat and sipped water Gavin had liberated from the suite's fridge. On the table in front of her was a nearly empty plate of crackers, cheese and chocolate he'd also found.

They only needed to make it, to hide, until cell service was restored. Until help could arrive.

Until.

Probably not *until* the storm subsided.

They were in for a long rest of the afternoon and night.

Gavin paced in from the bedroom, took a cracker and a piece of cheese then paced the length of the windows before he popped them in his mouth.

"Still nothing?"

He touched the phone at his hip with his elbow but shook his head. "Not even roaming. The tower must be out."

From the storm or Roy?

They had the same question about the road.

Storm or Roy?

"Maybe you should settle, lay down even. Catch a little bit of sleep."

He hadn't had much the night before. She knew that. Now she knew why. Her shields.

What she didn't know, didn't want to ask, was whether it was only *her* shields or all shielding.

He shook his head, rubbed at his neck.

"You're about to drop where you stand. With luck, he thinks we're gone. That we got away." She sipped her water. "I promise to wake you if I feel anything."

Those grey, stormy eyes met hers. "Anything at all?"

"Yes."

"I could do for thirty minutes or so." He pulled his weapon from the small of his back, sat on the couch, a few feet from her, and tucked the gun under his thigh but in easy reach. Then he leaned back, his head cradled by the overstuffed cushion and wiped a hand over his closed eyes. After several moments his breathing evened out.

She took another sip of water and turned her gaze to the window and the incoming storm.

GAVIN WOKE WITH a start.

He stayed where he sat, head cushioned against the back of a couch, a blanket tucked around his body and his gun under his thigh.

Darkness surrounded him. Rain pelted glass a few feet away.

And Calea's earthy, sensuous scent washed over him.

Stand down.

"What time is it?" His voice, low and raspy, echoed in the room.

"Seven." Her voice came from the direction of the chair.

He'd been asleep for several hours.

Her shields were still up, still pressed down on him, even when he knew she'd secured them into the walls. No alarms.

And he'd slept.

Deeply.

He straightened, twisted his head side to side, and groaned at the creaks and pops. *Conked out didn't cover it.* "I need to check the phone connection."

"Still down."

Shit.

"Since they are, and no one has been anywhere near this room or even this floor, I let you sleep."

"Did you drug my water?"

He felt her smile. "Not a chance."

An answering smile stretched across his mouth as he leaned against the back of the couch.

They needed to decide if staying here was the best option but it felt *nice* to semi-relax, even if just for this moment. Across the table separating them, he heard Calea stand. Stretch. Then she skirted the table and sat on the couch. Less than a foot separated them.

Awareness skittered over his skin.

The scent of her, that earthiness, surrounded him in the darkness. Filled him, even as the storm tossed waves against the rocks below the windows and rain beat against the glass.

"Calea –"

"I'm not a fool, Gavin." She trailed the tip of one finger down his bare forearm. "I will let you protect me, even let you take me back to the Institute. Let you leave me there. But I won't be waiting for your return. Whatever is between us will be over. Done."

The finality of her words, her tone, tightened his throat. His chest.

He could turn on a light. Look into her eyes. But somehow, right now, that didn't feel like a good option. Not when he knew he wouldn't like the conviction in her eyes that he could hear in her voice.

She leaned forward, the sweater covering her breasts soft against his arm, and her lips warm at his ear. "So, right now, for me, I'm taking this. Tell me now if you want me to stop."

He angled his head, met her mouth with his own.

Hunger, never far away where she was concerned, welled. Blocked his mind, his reasoning. Filled his groin. Her lips parted and he devoured. Her tongue met his, stroke for stroke.

Her hands cupped his face.

God, too many clothes separating them.

He gripped her shoulders, pulled her forward until she twisted and lay in his arms, across his lap, her mouth still glued to his and her hands linked behind his neck, holding him close to her.

If his desire wasn't already evident, it was now.

From under his thigh he retrieved his gun, leaned further forward to slip it under the couch, out of their way, before he angled his head for deeper access to her mouth. He ran his hand down her back then eased his hand under the hem of her sweater to tease the material upwards, his fingers glancing over her warm, soft skin until he cupped her breast through the lacey material of her bra.

Her breath caught and she angled her head away from his mouth to arc into him, those breasts tight against his chest.

"Calea." He squeezed, lightly, as he brushed his lips over her cheek. "This is crazy."

"You want me." She arched her neck. "I want you."

"There's a mad man out there –"

"Who doesn't know where we are." She wrapped her hands over his, urged him to pull her sweater over her head.

He did her bidding then set the sweater to the side before he ran his fingers through her hair, undoing the last of her braid. Each movement slow and torturous, he ran the tip of a finger over the lace cupping her breasts. "You're sure you want this? Like this? I won't make promises –"

"I'm not asking for any, am I?"

"No, you're not." He slipped the fingers of both hands under her bra straps and slid them down her arms before he skimmed his hands over her back and undid the hooks. The bra fell forward and he pulled it away from her then filled his palms with her breasts. "Calea."

He kneaded the sides as he bent forward and suckled a nipple. Her soft gasp went straight to his groin. Already hard, to the point of painful, he scraped his teeth over the tip of her rigid nipple.

Her hands, now at the bottom of his shirt, shoved it up his chest and her mouth latched onto *his* nipple, her tongue lathing that sensitive point. Then she twisted until she straddled his legs, her fingers into his waistband. "Unbutton them."

"Bossy, aren't you?" With one hand between their bodies, he undid the buttons of his jeans.

She slipped her hands inside his pants, and pushed his underwear down far enough to release him then she ran her fingers over him, under him, around him.

"Calea."

"You're saying my name an awful lot." Her low chuckle brought a growl from deep in his chest.

"I *like* your name." Damn, *sexy* woman. "But you're wearing too many clothes, *Calea*."

"Hmmm. I am, aren't I?" She wrapped her fingers tighter around him and squeezed once.

"Dammit, woman –"

"Make love to me, Gavin. Now. In the dark."

God, Calea. I do love you. In the dark. The light of day. So much, it hurt more than anything in his miserable life.

He wrapped his arms around her, pulled her close, bare skin to bare skin, before he rubbed his cheek over her hair and lay her down on the couch. There, he undid her pants and slid them and her panties down her legs. "Your skin is so soft."

"Come here and show me how hard you are."

"Keep talking like that, woman, and you're going to drive me to the edge." He shoved his own pants down and kicked them aside.

"That's right where I want you." She ran her bare foot up his leg, hooked it behind his knee. "On the edge, inside me."

"Funny, that's exactly where I want to be." He stretched out over her, settled between her legs and pressed his mouth to her neck. To the pulse throbbing there, for him.

Darkness surrounded them. Rain continued to beat against the glass. But there was only them. Only her. Only this stolen moment in time.

He lifted his hips, entered her in one hard stroke.

She gasped and arched upwards, her legs wrapped around his waist, meeting him, joining him in the hard, fast pace he set. Their bodies slick against each other, their rhythm desperate as they each reached for what the other offered. As they each filled the empty space inside the other.

This was theirs.

Here.

Now.

She climaxed around him, her body tightening and shuddering from the force. He let go, joining her as his own body shook from the power unleashed between them.

Two bodies. One heart.

Soul mates.

Whether he wanted it or not.

Chapter Eight

D RESSED AGAIN, GAVIN sat on the couch, his hands behind his head, while he waited for Calea to return from the bathroom where she'd escaped to set herself to rights. Of a sort. He kind of liked her hair mussed and her lips swollen.

Probably a male thing.

He ran a hand over the top of his head.

Dammit. He'd made a bad choice, making love to her in the dark.

No promises.

But she'd made one.

I won't be waiting for your return. Whatever is between us will be over. Done.

How the hell was he going to deal with the reality of that?

Outside the hotel window the night was as dark as before, although the rain seemed to have lessened to no more than a light drumming against the glass. The storm wasn't over, but it appeared to have lulled for the time being.

They still needed to decide if they should stay put and wait out the night or try for the Hummer and the road.

"We should regroup. Figure —" Calea stopped underneath the archway between rooms and frowned. "What is that noise?"

Underneath the beat of rain was a steady drone that had nothing to do with the storm.

Crap. "Turn off the bathroom light."

She spun to do as he asked then hurried, in the darkness, towards him. "What is it?"

"Get down." He dove towards her, taking his gun with him, and yanked her on top of him. Then he rolled them into a tight ball between the chair and the couch just as a beam of light refracted and bent through the panes of the windows.

Beneath him, both her hands pressed against his chest, she shivered. "What is that?"

"Helicopter with a search light." *Possibly a* stolen *helicopter with a search light.* The one Mac had mentioned.

She pushed at him. "Maybe that's your pilot. Or Ben."

"And maybe it's not."

"But if it is, could they be flying into a trap? An ambush?"

"Why would either of them be spotlighting this floor?"

Against his chest she shook her head.

"Hush." He pressed his lips to her temple. "We need to be still."

The thump of the helicopter's blades sounded as if they were right outside the window.

The light, brighter this time, swept the room again.

Shit.

Could whoever that was see anything in here, anything he and Calea didn't want seen? With the way the bathroom had been situated, out here its light had been dim and had barely illuminated the hallway between the rooms. Had it been bright enough to be seen before they'd heard the helicopter? Before Calea had shut it off?

He didn't think so. Hoped not.

His fingers tightened around the butt of his gun.

Did the room appear occupied or empty?

And why the hell was *this* room a target?

Why now?

The light shifted away, the pitch of the helicopter's whine changed.

"How would Roy get a helicopter? Unless the road's been repaired." Her soft breath feathered along his jaw. "But *why* would Roy get a helicopter?"

She pushed at him, wiggled beneath him.

His body reacted immediately.

No time.

One hand flat on the carpet, he pushed himself away and off her, missed the contact. "No idea."

"I still hear it." She scrambled to her knees. "It's still out there."

He nodded. "Maybe they're checking the other rooms."

"They. As in more than just Roy."

"Unless he knows how to fly a helicopter and had that bird stashed."

Too many unknowns.

"Come on. Time we bailed." He tucked his gun in his waistband at the small of his back and crouched low. They'd exit through the connecting doors to the suite to the immediate right. If whoever was in the helicopter *had* seen anything, that person would focus on this room. Not that one.

The darkness made it hard to navigate, but keeping low they managed to get to the other side of the room. He didn't dare turn on the penlight he had in his pocket, not with those drapes wide open. Once he reached the connecting door, he straightened and pressed his ear to it.

Silence on the other side.

Even the helicopter seemed quieter, as if it moved up and away from them.

With the chair he'd shoved under the doorknob earlier moved, he unlocked the door and inched it open. Here, he angled his body to block the other connecting locked doorknob from being seen and pulled the penlight then handed it to Calea to hold so he could see what he needed to do.

Simple.

Easy to get past.

The lock clicked and the door opened.

Success.

Behind them a soft thud hit the window.

Gavin pulled his gun as he spun and shoved Calea behind him.

Glass shattered. The entire wall of windows caved inward. The rush of angry wind and the sound of waves crashing against the rock below filled the room as the glass collapsed forward and scattered across the floor.

One man, no more than a shadow, swung into the room to land with a thump.

Gavin hit the wall switch, flooded the room with light and stood, legs braced, one foot behind the other, with his gun up and sighted on the man crouched on the floor. "Hands where I can see them."

Amid the shards of glass, a rope tight in his grasp, the man raised his head.

Hoffman. Dressed completely in black, broad shouldered and obviously fit. Light, as if glittering across the broken glass, flicked across his dark eyes. There, then gone.

Intent. *Take the woman.* There, then gone.

Gavin's grip tightened on his gun. *Like hell.* He aimed higher, at the man's head.

Hoffman let go of his rope and held up black gloved hands, palms forward. "All I want is Callie."

"Not happening."

"Be reasonable, Mr. Dunbar." Hoffman, hands still in the air and his movements slow, stood. He took a step forward.

"Don't move."

"You won't shoot me."

"Like hell I won't." Gavin let a humorless smile touch his mouth. "Single bullet. Forehead. End of problem"

Silence. Then Hoffman's chin lifted. "No one has to die."

"Your choice."

"Right." Condescendence coated the man's voice. "As if a senator's son would want the scandal involved."

"I don't give a shit about scandal. Maybe you should try doing more than a cursory search when you're prying into someone's life."

"Calea, if you come with me, I will let Mr. Dunbar live."

Calea not *Callie.* The implications of Hoffman's knowledge settled rock hard in Gavin's gut.

"Gavin can take of himself."

Good girl.

He didn't dare look at her. She was behind him, just inside the other room, and right now he blocked Hoffman's access. Gavin could back through the door, get it locked before the other man could rush him, but was that any real deterrent?

Hoffman had a gun. They knew that, had seen it earlier.

And a locked hotel door was no match for a bullet.

Dammit. No back up coming and he had no idea whether Hoffman worked for Milford, was a loose cannon, or both. Nor did Gavin have any idea how to contain the situation. "Keep your hands high. Move two steps to your right then sit, cross-legged on the floor."

"I don't think so." Hoffman's chin lifted.

Gavin shifted slightly, settled more comfortably into his shooting stance.

The other man's eyes glittered again. His own posture shifted. Not much, his hip a half inch to the left.

Enough.

Gavin lowered his aim, pulled the trigger as the man lunged forward.

A loud howl rent the space between them.

Must've hit the bastard.

Not pausing, Gavin backed into the other room, slammed the door shut and the lock home.

"This table." Calea tossed the skinny base of a shade-less, wrought iron table lamp on the king bed and shoved at a heavy writing desk that sat next to the door. Between the two of them, they had it in front of the connecting door in a matter of moments. She grabbed the lamp base again, held in it front of her like a club. "Now what?"

"Out and down the stairs."

Hoffman would be busy, for a few minutes at least, tending to his wound. Gavin had no illusions about the shot. He'd aimed for the knee, hopefully bad enough to slow him down.

The connecting door behind them shook.

Dammit to hell. He should have aimed higher.

Already moving toward the room's front door, he grabbed one of Calea's hands. "Bring your lamp."

"Wasn't leaving it here." As she met his steps stride for stride, she spun the base a half turn and tucked it under her arm. "Let's go, cowboy."

At the door, he paused long enough to look out the peephole, check the perimeter as well as he could, then eased open the door.

Hoffman had two choices. Take down one of the two barricades he and Calea had fashioned or come through the connecting door. After the way the door had shook, Gavin was betting on the connecting door.

A thud sounded behind them and that door vibrated again.

The writing desk slid an inch or so forward.

No time left.

Gavin tugged on Calea's hand. They slipped out through the room's front door into the hallway as another thud shook the room behind them and wood cracked.

The door frame or the desk, he had no idea.

Wasn't hanging around to find out.

How the hell they were getting out of here in one piece, he also had no blasted idea.

But standing here wasn't conducive to staying alive.

And he hadn't come all this way to protect Calea to let anything happen to her now.

"STAIRS?" CALEA, ALREADY moving down the tenth floor hallway, gripped the wider end of the wrought iron lamp and tapped the skinny length of it tucked under arm with her elbow.

Might not be a gun or a knife or a sword, but it was what she had and *dammit*, she'd whack it upside Hoffman's arrogant head if she had too.

Providing Gavin didn't shoot the man again.

Right now, she had no issues with that.

None.

"Service elevator." Gavin's deep voice settled somewhere in the pit of her stomach.

"Right." She sprinted ahead of him, made the right turn as a loud, splintering crash echoed behind them. At the concierge door, she slipped in her key, yanked open the door and sidestepped to let Gavin through, then yanked the door closed behind her and twisted the lock.

Across the room he had the service door entrance open. Once they made it through the small kitchen to the elevator, he hit the down button.

Praise be, the doors slid open.

Both of them hurried inside and Gavin hit the parking structure level button.

One below the lobby.

The doors slid closed. The elevator moved. An eternity passed.

The elevator slowed.

Gavin stepped in front of her, his elbows close to his sides and his weapon up.

The elevator jerked to a stop and, after another eternity, the doors squeaked open.

He leaned forward. With only his head out of the elevator, he scanned the area. Then he motioned for her to follow him. They stepped out onto a semi enclosed level of the parking structure.

Mostly empty, with low intensity lighting, the structure's cement beams were higher than normal, probably to allow for delivery trucks, and the concrete pillars were wide enough to hide behind.

She swallowed and touched her elbow to the lamp she held under her arm.

Cold and dampness permeated the air, chilled her through the layer of her sweater. Standing water puddled in the low spots of concrete, with rain being blown in through the open sides of the structure. Although right here, they were protected from the wind.

"Vehicle's that way."

"Right. I guess it's a little late to ask if you have your keys."

"Never been so grateful for no valet."

She nodded, fell in behind him as he guided the way, staying as near the center of the structure as they could. They had to be vigilant.

A man was trying to grab her.

Again.

Either Roy wasn't working alone after all or she had the worst luck when it came to men obsessing over her.

Shivers coated her skin, her hands trembled.

They weren't safe yet, this wasn't the time to break down.

She could do that later.

Gavin, with the gun in his left hand, pulled the keys from his right pocket, shifted the weapon back.

Damned if she wasn't glad he was here, after all.

She touched his elbow and he looked back at her over his shoulder.

"We'll make it, Calea."

Her bottom lip between her teeth, she nodded. They *would* make it.

They had to.

"Hoffman brought his own." Gavin pointed toward a mess of rope attached to an open type cage in the far corner.

"The ropes?"

He nodded. "I noticed them last night. When Hoffman burst in, I'd wondered if he'd used these ropes."

"He came from the roof, didn't he?"

"Yes. By helicopter. Probably the one *possibly* stolen from the airfield."

"That's a lot of planning, just to grab me."

"He's definitely focused on you."

"And you think it has something to do with before? That Roy's working for Milford?"

"He called you Calea. Not Callie. What does that say?"

"I'm back to *why*?"

Gavin, his gaze scanning the area around them, shook his head. "Here's our chariot."

He stopped next to a camouflaged painted, rugged, dirty mustard and sage green colored, lifted Hummer H1, military style, with huge, gnarly tires, a black push bar attached to the front grill and off road lights mounted on the roof. The Hummer had been pulled through so it sat facing forward, ready to be started, put in drive and go.

Her eyes widened. "This isn't a *car*."

"Rented it from the owner of the air field. I wasn't in the mood to be picky and this is what he had."

"Not complaining. It's just not your normal style."

"What works, works. Climb in, sweetheart." The corner of his mouth lifted. "Let's blow this joint."

A low chirp and the doors unlocked. She opened hers and with one foot on the side rail, grabbed the passenger handle to haul herself into the seat. The slight scent of pine greeted her from a tree deodorizer hanging from a knob on the center console.

Across the structure, near the loading area and service elevator, a door slammed and the echo reverberated across the pavement.

Her heart thumped hard against her chest from the inside.

"Company." Gavin shoved his gun under his thigh then the key in the ignition. "Buckle up."

The engine purred when he twisted the key, but that was still more noise than then they needed.

With her belt on, hands braced on the dashboard, she stared out the short windshield as he let his foot off the clutch and the Hummer H1 inched forward.

Movement across the structure caught her eye.

Damn.

"There." She pointed straight ahead. Hoffman, in a limping lope, jogged in their direction.

Gavin flicked the switch for the headlights and then for the overhead lights on the bar on top of the vehicle, drowning the area in front of them in brilliant light. Hoffman stopped, held his forearm over his face. In his other hand he held a gun.

She swallowed.

Wonderful.

Gavin pressed his foot to the gas pedal and the Hummer leapt forward. Tires squealed and Hoffman leapt to the side.

Something pinged the door of the driver's side.

Once.

Twice.

"Gavin?" She angled her body towards him.

"I'm fine. Bullets must have glanced off the door."

Her hands still braced on the dashboard, she spared a quick glance at the side mirror. Hoffman stood staring after the Hummer, his gun lifted, the barrel pointing upwards.

Gavin yanked the steering wheel and they sped to the left and out of the parking structure.

Rain immediately slammed into the vehicle, doused the windshield in a torrent.

Bright, blinding light from the vehicle's overhead running lamps reflected back against the rain and nothing except the short length of the hood was visible.

From one danger pit right into the bowels of another, with the manmade one hot on their heels. And all she could do was hang on and ride it out.

Chapter Nine

CALEA, SITTING FORWARD on the passenger seat, held a hand in front of her face at the brilliance of the light reflected back against that drenching wall of rain as they barreled away from the hotel parking structure.

In the driver's seat next to her, Gavin flipped on the wipers and reached for the knob that controlled the overhead bar lights.

The Hummer slipped, slid to the right.

Calea gasped, clutched at the dash.

A quick turn into the skid and they straightened.

Gavin yanked the knob of the overhead lights to off and suddenly they could see past the hood, into the darkness of the rain soaked night. In the narrow beam of their headlights, water swelled in front of them making the road look more like a wild river than a road of asphalt.

Her heart beat in time to the wipers, a fast and steady thump, one that couldn't keep up with the rain at all.

Now that they had a direction – straight – the gnarly tires drank greedily at the water, spit it to the side.

She swallowed against the lump tight in her throat. "Where to?"

Gavin shot her a sideways glance then his gaze fixed back through the windshield. "If the road's still out we'll be sitting ducks if we head that way."

"We could find a side road, under some trees, tuck in until morning."

"That's a possibility." In the glow from the dials, a muscle in his cheek twitched. "Might be the best possibility."

But he didn't like it. Didn't like running.

But what choice did they have?

"Hoffman will be following. I don't think in the helicopter. Not now that the storm's really kicked in." Gavin's gaze flicked to the rearview mirror, then back to the road. "Once he discovers we're not at the closure, he'll be backtracking. We need to make it difficult to find us."

"So we need some kind of camouflage?"

He nodded. "That and we take as many turns as possible. Nothing straight or predictable."

Lost so we can't be found.

For several minutes she stared out the windshield as the Hummer drank up the road. Ahead, to the right, appeared to be a dip in the overgrown foliage. She pointed. "Is that a side road? Or just a driveway"

He slowed to almost a crawl.

Sure enough, a narrow, paved lane angled away to disappear in darkness.

"It's not a dirt road." Humor laced the seriousness of Gavin's voice.

"Which, in these conditions, would be a *muddy* road."

"Four wheel drive. Big tires. We'd be fine."

"If you say so."

"Where's your sense of adventure?" He took the right turn.

"I'm here, aren't I?"

"Necessity. Not sure that translates to sense of adventure."

"Get me out of this, in one piece, and we'll talk about that."

His low chuckle warmed her from the inside.

Stop. None of this means anything. Not this flutter inside from those sideways glances, not the heat from his touch and *not* the love they'd made such a short time ago.

A quick, lifetime ago.

Once this was over, once he'd left her at the Institute, they were done. Finished. No more waiting on him. No more anything. At all.

His mind, his decisions, hadn't changed. *Remember that.* Especially when those stupid flutters spread molten heat through her belly.

She folded her hands over her stomach. She and Gavin were cocooned, together, inside this vehicle while the outside world stormed around them. They depended on each other, for now.

This was temporary.

She needed to concentrate on what was outside that windshield.

And Roy Hoffman was somewhere out there. Wanting only God knew what.

Gavin eased the Hummer forward along the lane as it bore to the left, then the right and back left, a sweep of gentle curves with wild foliage, dark and looming, pressing in on either side as the path narrowed.

And there was the constant beat of rain against the windshield. The roof.

"I hope no one is heading towards us on this road." She pressed her hands against the dash and leaned forward to peer through the rain. "I don't think another vehicle would fit. There's been nowhere to turn around."

"With this storm, I doubt anyone else, except Hoffman, is out tonight." Gavin eased the vehicle into another sweeping curve. "And unless he has some kind of tracker on us, on the Hummer, and there's a shortcut to where we are, he's not in front of us."

Well hell. "If that was supposed to be comforting, big fail."

"Simply stating things as I see them." In the glow from the gauges Gavin's cheek twitched. "Once this storm subsides, I imagine Hoffman will have that helicopter in the air again."

"So we need to not be findable."

"Piece of –"

"Don't." She held one hand up. "Bad things happen when one of us says that."

His chuckle washed over her skin.

Her insides fluttered. Again. *Well hell on that, too.*

"Shit." He leaned forward, closer to the steering wheel, eased up on the gas pedal and shifted into neutral. They coasted to a stop.

"What?" Leaning further forward, she flattened her palms against the dashboard, strained to see what he'd seen.

There, right in front of them, through the wall of rain, a dark wall of foliage, taller than the Hummer, stretched in both directions.

Hard hitting rain sluiced down the windshield. The wipers didn't stand a chance. Mud swirled in front of them.

She looked out her side window at the muddy ground, barely illuminated by the peripheral glow of the Hummer's headlights, surrounding their front tires. Shit was right. "I'm guessing we found your dirt road."

"Looks that way. Left or right?"

"Can I choose neither direction?"

"Sure. We'll just sit here and wait for dawn."

"Okay. But turn off the headlights and keep your foot off the brakes. Too easy to spot us."

That damn chuckle twisted her insides.

"Seriously. If we take that road, won't we leave ruts in the ground, ruts Roy can track us by? Right up to the spot where we're stuck in the mud and can't get out."

"Such little faith."

"I have plenty of faith. Just not in that road."

"Suggestions?"

"Go back the way we came?"

He nodded, sat staring out the windshield. Then he set the parking brake, pulled his penlight out of his pocket and rolled his window down a few inches.

Cold, damp air rushed in, mixing the scent of rain with wet earth and briny ocean.

The roar of waves crashing against rock, close by, and wind howling its way through the rain, filled the vehicle.

Elemental, biting and wild.

"Gavin, you're going to get soaked."

"Probably." Through the open part of the window, he aimed the thin beam of light up the muddy road then back along the thick hedge of foliage. After several sweeps of his light, he rolled the window up and once again they were ensconced in a dark cocoon. He wiped at the rain water dripping down his face. "Earlier I spotted a small break in those vines. For now, we turn around and see if we can find that break. Pray it's big enough to back into."

"Okay." She glanced out the windshield. Nodded once. As good a plan as any.

He handed her his light. "I'll go slow, let the head-lights do most of the work. When we find that spot, we'll need to do what I just did."

"Let's do it."

ONCE GAVIN GOT the vehicle turned around, he eased it forward back along the paved road. The opening he thought he'd spotted couldn't be too far back. Calea sat in her seat, the fingers of one hand tucked in the collar of her sweater near the base of her throat, the other with his penlight, sweeping across the hedge of vines along her side of the vehicle.

Damp, chilled air swept in through her partially opened window.

"There." A slight spike of adrenaline edged her voice.

He stopped the Hummer. Leaned closer to her. Breathed in the flowery scent of her hair as his gaze followed the sweep of her light.

Sure enough.

A break in the foliage. Although the top was tangled together to make a roof of sorts, the sides tapered to a wide opening at the ground level. Almost like a cave inside the vines. Tailor made for their needs at this moment. Might not be quite as wide as the Hummer, but definitely as high as the vehicle was tall. He'd back the Hummer in, make it fit, pay the owner for a new paint job once this was over. "Let's do it."

COCOONED INSIDE THE Hummer, bundled in the blankets she and Gavin had found when they rummaged through the utility locker when they'd climbed through and explored the vehicle, Calea snuggled down in her front passenger seat.

They'd also found water and some kind of weird tasting rations they'd shared. No complaints, though. Her belly was full. They were both reasonably dry.

Considering.

The night still stretched out in front of them. They had no idea where Roy was, but the Hummer was well hidden, several yards off the road and tucked in the bramble.

Outside, the storm still surged. Still blew a hard rain practically sideways. Not as cold as it could have been, the lowered clouds held some warmth in the night air in addition to the closeness of the vine thicket surrounding three sides of the Hummer. Not a lot of warmth, but it wasn't freezing.

With the trees overhead and the bramble on each side, they were as snug as they could be without four walls and a heater. Besides, she was used to Minnesota winters. This was nearly balmy in comparison. If she ignored the damp, humidity factor.

And she was going to keep telling herself that.

She pulled the edges of the blanket tighter, glanced at Gavin, who sat in the driver's seat, his own blanket loose around his shoulders and the glow from the screen of his cell phone illuminating the frustration marring that rugged face.

"Still no reception?"

"None." He flicked a sideways glance at her. "We'll be here a few hours at least. Recline your seat and rest."

She should.

But her mind was entirely too active right now.

And her body too aware of Gavin. "Tell me about your mother."

His gaze, sharp and full of caution in the illuminated light, locked on hers. "Don't psycho-analyze me, Calea."

"I'm not asking as an analyst."

"Right. Just as a concerned friend."

"Wasn't that what you wanted? Us to be *friends*?"

Dammit. Going there hadn't been her intent.

His mouth tightened.

She turned to face forward, leaned her head back on the seat's headrest and stared out the windshield into the darkness. "So you don't want me as a friend. You don't want me as your lover. There's no way we can go back to being mere acquaintances. Where does that leave us?"

"I never said I didn't want you, Calea."

She twisted the edges of the blanket tighter, closer, and squeezed her eyes closed, just for a moment. No, he wanted her. Just didn't *want* to want her. How could such simple words hurt so damn much? Where was her damn resolve? From under her lashes she glanced at him. "Gavin –"

The glow from his phone reflected a banked heat in his eyes, there then gone as the screen went dark.

Pressure constricted her chest.

God, being near him *hurt* like hell.

And she'd be damned if she'd again ask where that left them. Especially since she knew the answer was *nowhere*. "About your mother."

His sigh, heavy in the air, stroked every inch of her skin, sent prickles down her spine. Stirred heat in places she didn't want stirred.

She straightened her spine, threaded her fingers through her loose hair, and shook it back. Anything to give herself time to think.

This close to him, this intimate, the desire to run her hands under that blanket, under his shirt and over his naked chest, was close to being her undoing. A pain so intense she could practically touch it.

She clenched her hands in her damp hair, at her nape.

What did the link between them look like? She'd asked her grandmother before, more than once, but Mimi would never answer. She'd just give her that sly smile while a wicked light danced in her hazel eyes, eyes so much like Calea's.

Had that link between Calea and Gavin stretched? Thinned out to almost non-existence?

A golden flicker flashed across her inner vision. There then gone.

Right.

There was that. That burgeoning possibility of his future with someone else.

Another slash of deep pain to her already aching heart.

Focus on something else. Anything else. "Your mother?"

"You're not going to let it go."

"Depends on what else you want to talk about."

He stirred in his seat. Shifted. Silence stretched for a long moment. "My mother was, at one time, an amazing woman. Funny, loving. When I was young, she seemed so full of adventure. Full of life. The center of my father's world. So much so, there were times he hardly seemed aware of me."

"He loved her?"

"My father isn't a *nice* man." Derision coated his words. "Add in an irrational obsession and I'm not sure what he felt for her was love."

Her fists still at her nape, she angled her head so her left cheek pressed against the inside of her lower arm and waited.

"But they both called it that. Even when he screamed at her because another man looked at her sideways. When he was so sure that man or some other one was going to steal her away. When he'd smack her across the face because he'd convinced himself she was having an affair. She was his and she wasn't getting away from him."

Oh. "Why did she stay?"

"I asked her once. In front of him."

"So, you've always been a bit reckless."

"I'd just entered my teens. Full of myself. Sure of my place in the world." The sneer in Gavin's voice was unmistakable. "Sure my father was the biggest ass to ever live. The way he treated my mom – she should have left him."

"What happened when you asked her why she stayed?"

"My father became completely aware of me in that moment. I had no idea I'd painted a huge red target on my back. My mother knew. Turns out, as I found out later, according to my grandmother, she'd always tried to protect me. Always kept me wrapped tight in a protective shield meant to deflect the worst of his awareness."

Shields. Smothering. Suffocating. "This is what she did instead of leaving him? Wrapped you in a silk sheath to block his bad intentions from you? Or to keep you off his radar?"

"Both. But that day, when I confronted her, she said, right there in front of him, she couldn't leave him. Wouldn't ever leave him. That she was *fated* to love one man. My father." The scruff of stubble along his jaw being rubbed echoed in through the darkness. "Then he backhanded me, told me to mind my own business and stay out of his."

"And your mother?"

"Sent me to my room."

"Away from him."

"That room fast became unbearable. Oppressive. So I escaped as often as I could."

"Her shielding?"

"Probably. My grandmother tried to tell me it was the only way my mother knew to protect me."

"You don't believe that."

"No. She should've left."

"Why do you think she didn't?"

She felt him shrug. Waited.

This time his sigh was self-directed. More internal than irritated. "The pat answer, the one most used, is that she stayed for me. Stability. Tearing the family apart would be selfish."

"And the real answer?"

"My grandmother believes it's because my mother actually *loved* the son of a bitch."

Although Calea had never met his grandmother, she knew the woman had her own following in the seer world, was nearly as famous as Mimi. And Gavin hadn't answered her question. "Maybe your mother did love him."

"And maybe, because she believed everything her mother force-fed her for all those years, she didn't see a future without him." A sneer coated each word. "If you're with your *soul-mate* and you leave him, what's left for you?"

Calea's stomach clenched in on itself. Damn good question. One she didn't have an answer to, not yet. "So she stayed because, what? She was afraid whatever else was out there would only be worse than what she had?"

"No. She was *positive* there wasn't anyone else out there for her."

"But that's not necessarily true."

"Really?" He touched a strand of her hair, stroked it. "You believe there's someone else out there for me? Someone besides you?"

Bastard. That golden glimmer she'd *seen* flitted through her mind. "There could be, yes."

"And someone else for you?"

Never. "Yes."

He rubbed the strand of her hair between his thumb and forefinger, brushed the palm of his hand over her forearm. "You'd make a life with someone else?" In the darkness his voice took on a hardened edge. "You'd forget me? Forget how we are, together?"

Bastard was too good a word for him, right now, at this point.

She swallowed once, resisted shaking her head and pulling her hair away from him. "I couldn't forget you.

Ever. Is that what you want to hear? But *you* turned away from *us*, so there is no us any longer. I'm not going to pine away, not going to piss away my life hoping you'll *someday* change your mind."

But wasn't that what she had been doing?

In essence?

"Is that what Mimi says?"

"I don't need Mimi to agree with me. It's my life."

"But does she? Agree with you?"

Where was he going with this? "Yes, she does."

He let go of her hair.

Shouldn't she be ecstatic? It was *hair*, but the loss of his touch left her isolated. Adrift. Like she'd lost him all over again.

"My grandmother should've given her daughter that same advice. That same support."

"From what I understand, she and Mimi don't always see eye to eye on this stuff."

"If my mother had left my father, she'd still be alive."

"You implied yesterday that he was somehow responsible for your mother's death." She had to choose her words carefully here. "Literally? Or –"

"Literally."

Oh.

"But I can't prove it."

"How do you –" *Oh, Lord.* "You *read* your father's intent."

"The first time I consciously remember *reading* anyone, it was my mother's intent to confront my father on

114

something." Frustration lined Gavin's voice. "I have no idea on what. The knowledge was just there. Confront and pray he didn't realize she was bluffing."

Calea pulled her bottom lip between her teeth.

"It had been a couple years, but I was still a teenager. Still pretty full of myself. I told her that whatever it was she was up to, bluffing wouldn't work with him. He'd see through her in an instant.

"Then, maybe a week later, he hauled me into his office for some offense I was probably guilty of, and I *read* him." Gavin's voice tightened. Roughened. "*She was his,* dammit*, and she'd die before he let her go.*"

"But –"

"My mistake was in confronting him. Again, that teenage arrogance. I *read* him but had no idea he was completely serious. That realization, that he was in fact willing to kill her if it was the only way to prevent her from leaving him, came later. I do know I freaked him out. After all, I am my grandmother's grandson. So he accused me of all sorts of things, the least of which was actually reading his mind. And that gave him the perfect excuse to pick a fight with my mother.

"Mom slammed out of the office and my father followed. But not before he stared right at me, his intent completely obvious to me. I ran after him, after them. But Mom had taken the car and my father followed in his. It was ruled an accident. I was a teenager who'd witnessed a horrendous fight between his parents just before his mother died. I was distraught. And wrong.

According to the authorities. It was an accident. My mother's fault. And I couldn't prove him responsible."

"He got away with it."

"And has hated me ever since."

"Gavin —"

"Regardless of what kind of man my father was, she believed she was *fated* to be with him. Until the day she died. And she was. Literally."

"Bad things, bad people, they exist." Dammit, Calea pressed a hand over her heart. Rubbed. He *knew* this. Dealt with it on a constant basis. But good people also existed. "Bad decisions are made. And sometimes we throw fate in when we don't want to face our own part in those bad decisions."

"Screw fate."

"Obviously you are."

"My grandmother *believes* Mom loved that asshole so much, so completely, she couldn't be with anyone else. Explosive passion that filled her and left no room for another love."

"Gavin —"

"I can't do that to you, Calea. To me. To us."

"I'm not you're mother, Gavin."

"This *desire* that ignites between us, burning so hot it consumes every coherent thought in my head, pushing me to touch you when I know I shouldn't? That *desire* tells me *you're mine*. That says I am my father's son, Calea."

"No. That doesn't make you your father."

"Doesn't it? When I first arrived here, my first incli-
nation was to grab you, to demand to know why the hell
you'd run from where I knew you'd be safe. Not only
from Milford, but from other men seeing you. Wanting
you. And safe from me. Safe from my obsession with
you."

"You want me wrapped in that silk sheath, like your
mother did to you."

"Damn straight. And I don't give a crap how that
sounds. I wanted to rip Hoffman's arm off for being in
the same room with you. For feeling he had the *right* to
touch your shoulder that way."

"Because you love me?" Her stomach in a tight knot,
she stared ahead, through the dark windshield.

He shifted in his seat, settling further against his
door. Further away from her. "Because I'm *obsessed* with
you."

Not the same thing at all.

He didn't have to say the words for his meaning to
ring loud in her head.

"You should get some sleep while you can." His
voice, devoid of all emotion, echoed around the stripped
confines of her heart.

With no idea what to say, or how to say anything
without her voice breaking, she curled against her own
door and hugged the blanket tight around her shoulders.

Chapter Ten

GAVIN, HIS ARMS tight around Calea's relaxed body, shifted in his seat, careful not to wake her. His chin rested on the top of her head and loose tendrils of her hair tickled his neck, caught in the scruff along his jaw, but he ignored that as he stared out the windshield of the Hummer.

Morning had just begun to creep over the horizon and the storm had dissipated to a light drizzle. Sometime during the night, in her sleep, she'd found her way into his arms. Since he wasn't about to push her away, he held her and waited.

Last night's honesty had taken its toll and while he'd managed to catnap, even with Calea's shields in place, he wasn't rested by any means.

Nor did he have any answers.

What the hell did Hoffman want with Calea? Had Milford sent him? If so, what did Milford want?

Round and round.

Pertinent to their current situation, but also a way to not dwell on his parents.

Their relationship.

His own obsession.

Calea had said she wasn't his mother. True. But that same fire was there, underneath. That same sense of loyalty. Warm. Loving. If he'd given her the chance, would Calea have made different choices than his mother had? Would she stand by him even if it meant he might eventually be the cause of her death?

How could he allow her to risk that? Much less ask it of her.

But how was he going to walk away? Let her find that other man to make a life with? Have babies with.

His arms tightened around her and he buried his face in her hair.

"Mmmm." She stirred, curled into him then rubbed her cheek against the blanket separating their bodies. "Gavin."

"Morning."

She stiffened in his arms.

Pushed at his chest.

Reluctant, he loosened his grip, let his arms fall away as she scrambled back to her side of the Hummer. She sat there, her own blanket loose around her body, her eyes wide and slightly unfocused. All that wavy hair mussed around her face and shoulders.

With the back of her hand, she rubbed her mouth, angled her head to stare out the windshield.

"I could use a stretch, a nature break." He kept his voice low. Friendly.

A bare trace of a smile touched her lips. "Coffee would be good."

"There's water."

"That'll do." She ran her tongue over her teeth. "Toothpaste?"

"There's some of that, too."

"What are we waiting for?"

"You to test our boundaries."

"Already done." She ran her fingers through her hair. Shook it back from her face.

He followed her movements, blinked when she caught his gaze and a shutter fell over hers. What had he expected? "Nothing out there?"

"Nothing at all. Seems almost too still."

He scanned the area through the windshield again. Unless Hoffman took the helicopter up and had excellent binoculars or happened by this spot, they should be invisible. And if either of those happened, they should be able to hear him coming.

"Maybe it's the rain." She frowned. "Or that it's just now dawn."

"Maybe."

"No cell service yet?"

Gavin shook his head. None.

"Then let's answer nature's call and formulate another plan." Brambles scratched against the door as she shoved it open. "Where's that toothpaste?"

Ten minutes later, nature appeased and his own teeth cleaned, Gavin leaned against the Hummer's push-bar as Calea stood between him and the paved road, her legs braced and hands at her hips, staring at an extremely narrow trail that angled away through the thicket of overgrown vines.

The drizzle had turned to little more than mist. The soft, barely there, light caught the droplets and sparkled along the waves of her loose hair. He itched to run his fingers through all that hair, bury his face there at the juncture of her neck and shoulder. Breathe her in.

Not too far away waves hit the side of the cliffs, the sound muffled, but there.

Nature, a wild seething tempest, had nothing on him.

On what being near her did to his insides.

Leave it alone, Dunbar.

He shoved his hands into his front pockets, leaving his thumbs free. "What are you sensing?"

She shook her head. "Absolutely nothing."

"And that bothers you."

"Yes."

"Maybe we are all alone out here. It's pretty wild looking."

"This close to the coast of Oregon it stays wild looking, no matter how people try to tame it."

"So what's the issue?"

"Me." From the narrow thicket trail Hoffman stepped out to stand several feet from Calea.

She startled and stumbled backwards as Gavin, his gut suddenly tight, straightened, yanked his hands from his pockets and moved to grab the gun he had tucked at the small of his back.

"I don't think so, Dunbar." Hoffman, his dark eyes shadowed in the low morning light, aimed a long barreled, vicious looking rifle at Calea. "One wrong move and you know what happens."

"Nothing happens." Gavin, both hands still behind his back, eased his fingers around the butt of his gun. "You want her alive or she'd already be dead."

And although she was off to the side, she was between him and Hoffman.

"True." Hoffman, a blood soaked, makeshift bandage just above his knee, swung the barrel of his rifle towards Gavin. "You, however, I do want dead."

"Join the crowd." Gavin yanked his weapon from its position, tucked his shoulders forward. "Down, Calea."

He rolled forward as a bullet hit the windshield of the Hummer. One part of him tracked Calea's movements, knew she'd dropped and rolled to the opposite side of the thicket. He also rolled onto his back, brought his gun up and aimed at where Hoffman had been.

Empty space.

Shit.

He scanned the area as he twisted into a crouch.

Where the hell was Hoffman?

Slight movement caught at the corner of Gavin's eye, there inside the thicket.

He was an open target here, but he had to protect Calea. At all cost.

"Get back here, Calea, to the Hummer." With his weapon he tracked the movement behind the bramble as Calea scrambled backwards towards him and the vehicle.

"Gavin —"

"To the Hummer." He duck-walked those few feet backwards, his focus on the bramble and the movement that stopped.

Shit.

"Go." He threw himself to the side, keeping her between himself and the vehicle.

Another shot rang out, hitting the dirt inches from his face. A metallic taste tinged the air.

Too damn close.

He scrambled to his feet, grabbed Calea's arm and they shoved aside the thorny vines, ignored the scrapes to their skin, to tuck in behind the rear of the Hummer. Both breathing shallow and erratic, they squatted to keep their heads out of view of the back window, leaned against the vehicle, and shared a quick glance.

"Now what?"

"Dunbar." Hoffman's voice, from somewhere near the front of the vehicle, didn't sound as firm or confident as it had a short time ago. "You're right. I won't hurt Calea."

Gavin leaned his head back, listened for a moment for any kind of clue to where the man stood. Beside him, her face pale, Calea mirrored his posture.

"She can't get away from me." Hoffman's voice changed to a more conversational mode. "I'll find her, wherever she goes."

A definite hunter.

Question was, how the hell was he doing it? He hadn't found them by air and sure as hell hadn't driven by and spotted them.

As for tracking, Calea's shields should have blocked the man.

Gavin held a finger to his mouth. She nodded once.

Something, like a fist, hit the Hummer, the sound reverberating through the vehicle. "Dammit, Dunbar. Give her to me and I'll let you live."

Like hell he would.

The direction of Hoffman's voice was unquestionably from the front of the vehicle, the part that faced the road. From here at the back, considering the bramble of vines, and the fact they'd had to shove the Hummer into the opening, there was nowhere for them to go that wouldn't leave them wide open for target practice.

They were stuck.

The flipside was Hoffman had the same dilemma. As long as they could keep tabs on his whereabouts.

Question was, how long before Hoffman's patience wore thin and he tried to force the issue?

The Hummer shifted, the back lifting slightly.

Shit. He had his answer.

Hoffman was climbing over the top.

Gavin touched Calea's arm, pointed to the underside of the vehicle.

They needed to not be here once Hoffman made it to the back. And they didn't have much time.

Calea nodded and scurried underneath. He followed, his weapon in hand, as the vehicle rocked with Hoffman's weight. Together, Gavin and Calea doubled timed their belly crawl to the front of the Hummer.

She pulled herself out, twisted into a half crouch to face him.

"What the hell?" Hoffman's bellow echoed around them.

Not completely out from under the vehicle, Gavin rolled onto his back, scooted forward and, with both hands on the butt of his gun, aimed at the spot just over the roof of the Hummer.

Hoffman appeared and Gavin rested his finger on the trigger of his weapon.

Dark eyes no longer flat, Hoffman's blistering gaze locked on Gavin's. The man stopped.

"Throw your weapon down, Hoffman."

The man's mouth lifted into a snarl.

This was the person who'd torn Gavin's room apart two nights ago. Who had a rage so wild it was unpredictable.

"Hoffman. You have a count of two before I shoot you."

The man's top lip twitched and he growled.

"One."

Hoffman's gaze flicked to Calea.

"Two."

The rifle sailed into the air, landing with a thud on the dirt path behind them.

"Grab it Calea." Gavin heard her scramble for it. "Point it at him."

"Done."

With his elbows, and his gaze locked on Hoffman, he pulled himself the rest of the way out from under the Hummer. Once he stood, he backed several feet away from the vehicle, cupped the butt of his weapon with both hands and rested his index finger on the trigger as he aimed at Hoffman's tucked chin. "Why don't you join us down here?"

Hoffman snarled again but he yanked himself forward and slid off the hood of the vehicle to stand, legs shoulder width apart, favoring the leg with the bandage around it, a few feet from Gavin. The man's pallor was chalky and his breathing, erratic and shallow. His gaze flicked from Calea to Gavin then back to Calea.

"Hands on your head. Down on your knees."

A sneer covered Hoffman's mouth, nearly covering the slight tremble, but he linked his fingers together on top of his head. "Thanks to you, I have a wound in my thigh, I'm not going down to the ground."

"I can make it two for two." Gavin lowered his aim. "Then run your ass over and leave you to wait for the authorities."

"You'd do it, too."

"Damn straight. On your knees."

Hoffman's mouth thinned. He went down on his leg with the gunshot wound but kept the foot of his good leg flat on the ground.

"I said knees." Gavin shifted his aim, centering on the man's chest.

Again Hoffman's gaze flicked between him and Calea who now stood several feet to the side and behind Gavin.

"Nooooo." The man bellowed, shoved upwards.

Gavin, following Hoffman's movement, pulled the trigger but missed as the man suddenly threw himself sideways to roll towards Calea.

She shot her rifle, the bullet gouging the dirt inches from Hoffman as he rolled into her and knocked her to the ground. Gavin covered the few feet but came up short, hands lifted as Hoffman pulled Calea on top of him, rolled into a sitting position with Calea on his lap, her back against him. He held her snug with one hand around her waist and the other at her throat.

Over her head Hoffman met Gavin's gaze.

Madness leached out of the other man's eyes, leaving them dark, although the flatness marking him a mercenary hunter hadn't returned. His pasty pallor gone, his breathing was even and deep.

A sudden chill settled over Gavin's skin. *What the hell had just happened to Hoffman?*

A hint of arrogance touched the corners of Hoffman's mouth. "I don't want her dead, but I will hurt her if I have to. Your choice."

Gavin lowered his weapon slightly, cupped the butt of the gun but kept his trigger finger along the barrel and aimed at the man's head. "Or I could just shoot through her to get you."

He ignored the slight widening of Calea's eyes. She knew what to do. He had to believe that, otherwise she'd be struggling. Instead she was perfectly still.

Waiting.

"We both know you won't." Hoffman stroked Calea's neck and his eyelids fluttered, ever so slightly. "Toss the gun, Dunbar."

"We don't have to do this."

"Yes, I do."

Helicopter. Small, two-seater. Whisk Calea away.

Hoffman's intent. Plain and simple.

Gavin had to keep that from happening. He cross stepped a foot closer. "Why?"

The right edge of Hoffman's mouth lifted a fraction. "I will hurt her, Dunbar, if you insist on being a hero."

But he wouldn't kill her. That intent was also evident.

"Being a hero is what I do best." In less than a few seconds, Gavin shifted so that his right foot was braced behind, left foot forward and had his gun lifted to sight down the barrel at the other man's forehead. Just behind Calea's head.

"Shame about that." Hoffman smiled, full with teeth showing. He let go of Calea's neck.

She immediately hunched forward, giving Gavin a perfect shot. He took it.

That bullet hit the ground a moment after Hoffman rolled to the side and reached behind his back to come up with a gun.

How the hell had the man moved that fast?

A sharp pain seared across the outside of Gavin's left arm. He flinched, but strode forward, his weapon up and trained on Hoffman.

The man rolled again, with Calea struggling in his arms. He ended in a standing position, one arm around her waist and holding her off the ground with his gun pressed to her throat.

Son of a bitch. Gavin's top lip curled. He lowered his chin.

His arm stung, but it was only a slight graze. Didn't matter. He couldn't risk shifting his focus from the bastard who held Calea. "Put her down, Hoffman. You're not getting away."

Hoffman took a step backwards, then another. "I wouldn't be so sure about that, Dunbar. We both know you won't shoot her."

"Neither will you." Gavin moved those same two steps closer. "Looks like we're at a stand-off."

"Hardly."

"How do you figure?"

"I have more to lose. More at stake. Makes me more dangerous." A ghost of a smile crossed Hoffman's mouth. There, then gone. Hoffman took another step backwards, into the thicket of vines. Then another.

Gavin rotated his head, sighted down his weapon. Aimed at the man's forehead.

This had gone on long enough.

Time to end it.

Gavin took a quick breath, teased the trigger, and stood completely alone.

Hoffman had vanished.

And Calea with him.

Chapter Eleven

G AVIN STOOD COMPLETELY still.
And completely alone.

Gun raised and pointed at empty air.

Where the hell had Calea and Hoffman gone? Disappeared. Not possible. Even in a world full of impossibilities.

The only intent he'd read was the helicopter. Nothing about *vanishing*.

He scanned the bramble of vines in front of him, angled his head a slight bit to the left, then the right. Earlier, the first time he'd lost track of Hoffman, there had been movement in the thicket. Not enough to pinpoint the man, but enough so he knew Hoffman's general location.

No movement at all this time.

Nothing.

"Calea?" He teased his senses, rusty senses he rarely used. Stretched them.

The faint, metallic scent of blood hung in the air.

His? Or Hoffman's?

Gavin rotated his left shoulder, the ache in his arm burned. Hurt like a bitch. Nothing he couldn't ignore.

He pushed his senses out further. Wider.

There. Just there. Right in front of him, where Hoffman had stood holding Calea. Something off, but not off enough to raise any kind of alarm.

Like something was there but not there.

His gun still raised, he took a step forward. Then another.

Pain exploded through his injured arm and he spun around, flinching, as if someone had sucker punched him directly in the grazed wound. "Son of a bitch."

With his injured arm throbbing and warm, fresh blood dripping down his skin, he faced where the punch seemed to have come from, towards the road, with his back to the Hummer. "Calea?"

Still nothing.

"Hoffman?" Gavin again stretched out his senses, this time in the direction of the road.

Zilch.

Except …. He tilted his chin. Narrowed his eyes.

There.

A slight variation in the air. Again, right in front, between him and the pavement.

Now what?

If that variation was Hoffman, if – somehow – the man had figured out how to camouflage himself completely, Gavin still couldn't shoot him. Couldn't risk hitting Calea.

What the hell was he supposed to do now?

CALEA'S GAZE LOCKED on Gavin's arm. On the blood dripping down his skin.

Gavin. Dammit.

She arched against the hold Roy Hoffman had on her, his arm tight around her waist and holding her off the ground, one hand over her mouth. She butted her head against his chin.

He hissed then laughed in her ear. "He can't see you, Princess."

No shit.

She'd figured that one out on her own.

That was why she'd kicked Gavin as Roy had *strolled* around him. Only now Gavin was bleeding even more than before.

"He can't hear us, either."

She tried to head-butt Roy once more, but his hand tightened over her mouth and his fingers and thumb dug into her cheeks.

"Do that again and I'll kill him. Right here. Right now. Right in front of you."

She stilled at the ominous tone in his voice.

"Good girl." His breath stirred the hair in front of her ear, scraped across her skin. "We're going to back out of here, I'm going to put you down and we're both going to walk on down the road. Behave and I won't shoot Dunbar again."

She swallowed against the bile rising in her throat, against the scent of damp earth on Roy's hands.

"Understand?"

With her eyes closed, blocking out the sight of Gavin standing five feet away when he might as well have been fifty, she gave one quick nod.

She understood all right.

Both she and Gavin were screwed unless she came up with something, anything, to get away.

Right now she'd cooperate.

But only until she found an opportunity to not cooperate.

GAVIN, STANDING IN the center of the paved road in front of the Hummer, pushed out his senses once again.

That aberration was gone, as completely as if it had never existed.

He'd followed it a few feet but then lost the feel of it. Right now, he'd swear he was as alone as he appeared. Where the hell had they gone?

And how did he find them?

The main road had to still be out or his pilot would've called him. *If the phones worked.*

Lots of *ifs* and *maybes.*

Helicopter. Escape. He'd read that flash of intent off Hoffman.

The one from last night? At the hotel.

Was the helicopter still there? The roof was flat and Hoffman had rappelled down from there. Unless Hoffman had moved the helicopter since, the hotel was where the helicopter still sat.

And if not?

Gavin sucked in a lungful of briny, ocean filled air.

He'd tear the place apart, dig into Hoffman's employment records. Find an address.

His arm ached like a son of a bitch. He needed to wrap it, get back to the hotel.

Find Calea.

Put a bullet between Hoffman's eyes if he hurt her.

CALEA YANKED HER arm from Roy's loosened hold as they moved through the empty lobby of the hotel. He laughed but didn't reach for her.

Probably figured she had no real place to go, nowhere she could hide that he couldn't find her. Worst part, he was probably right.

She had no idea how to get away from him.

He blocked her attempts to mentally reach out to Gavin, to anyone else. Her shields didn't do a damn bit of good. He shredded them as if they were tissue paper thin.

She had no tricks left. No resources. No ideas.

So, instead, she stopped, right in the center of the open area.

Roy also stopped. His mouth tightened as he turned to her. "Let's go."

She shook her head.

"I will carry you if I have to."

"You're wounded." She waved a hand towards his leg. Fresh blood oozed across the dried, caked blood on the makeshift bandage. The blood also caked his black pants.

"Are you offering to play nurse?"

"Hardly." She crossed her arms over her stomach, lifted her chin. "Maybe I should make you carry me. With that wound you won't last long."

"Word of advice." He crossed his arms over his chest in a mirror of her posture. "Don't underestimate me."

Like she'd make that mistake again. "What do you want from me?"

"You to quit stalling. To quit making this so damn difficult." His hand snaked out and he gripped her arm. "Let's go."

"No." She yanked backwards, shocked when he let go of her. She stumbled a couple steps.

"Dunbar isn't going to make it in time."

Maybe Roy shouldn't underestimate Gavin, either. She hoped. Prayed. "In time for what?"

Roy ran a hand over his face then splayed both hands at his hips. But he didn't answer.

She stole a glance around the lobby. "Where is everyone?"

"Gone."

"Gone where?"

"Where they won't get in the way." His detached, cold voice matched his suddenly flat eyes.

Oh, shit. She swallowed but shook her hair back from her face. "You killed them."

"What difference does it make?"

"A lot."

"Why? You don't know any of them. Not personally."

"How do you know that?"

"Not one of them worked here the last time you stayed."

"Neither did you." Ice chilled her veins. "How do you know all of this? Why? What's really going on, Roy?"

"You ask a lot of questions."

"I'm just getting started."

He jerked his head, indicating the direction of the elevators. "Ask while we move."

"I'm not going anywhere else."

He grabbed her again, twisting her around to hold her back flush against his chest, both his arms clamped around hers and her middle. She struggled, kicked backwards, connecting with his shin. He didn't budge. Just tightened his grip. His breath fanned her cheek. "I don't want to hurt you, Calea. But I will if you make me."

She stilled at the dark, ominous undercurrent of his voice.

"No more fighting." He loosened his hold then slid one hand down her arm to wrap his fingers around her wrist. "No more struggling."

With a tug, he pulled her forward, towards the elevators. He punched the up button and the doors to the left slid soundlessly open.

Once inside, he hit the button for the top floor. As the doors closed he let go of her wrist.

She rubbed at the tender skin but wouldn't meet his gaze.

How the hell was she going to get away from him?

The elevator slowed, bumped to a stop and the doors opened.

She raised her eyes, met his flat gaze.

"I will hurt you if you try anything." He lifted a hand, indicated she exit first.

Tossing her hair back from her face, she spun away from him and moved into the hallway of the tenth floor.

A cold wind, sharp with the scent of the ocean, funneled down the hallway, swirled around her, whipped loose strands of her hair across her face. She shoved those away, behind her ears.

Debris, from a busted door, littered the floor in front of the room she and Gavin had occupied. Had it only been yesterday evening?

Gavin. Where was he? Had badly had he been hurt?

Blood from his wound dripping down his arm, eyes clouded in pain. Not seeing them.

"You camouflaged us." She turned to Roy. "Earlier. How were you able to do that?"

How was it even possible to do something like that?

"This way." Roy gripped her shoulder, turned her to face the direction of the stairs. Nudged her forward then dropped his hand when she moved toward the door. Once opened, he urged her into the stairwell.

Two steps up, she tried again. "Roy, how did you keep Gavin from seeing us out there?"

If she could get an answer, maybe she could formulate a game plan of some sort.

"Keep moving."

"Roy —"

"It's something I've perfected."

She hit the landing, turned toward him. "So you're not a null."

"Hardly." He indicated she head up the next set of steps.

"But –"

"Something else I perfected. Staying under the radar. Comes in handy. Keep moving."

There was another door at the top of the steps. Probably to the roof, considering they'd been on the top floor already. "Why are we going up here?"

"Do you ever stop asking questions?"

"No. You should probably get used to that." She hit the last landing, stopped just short of the door.

"Open it."

"What's out there?"

"Open the damn door."

"All right, already." She pressed the handle downward, pulled it toward her. The wind shoved the door, and her with it, inwards. If she hadn't been holding the handle, she'd have fallen. "Happy?"

His right arm above her, he held the door open and motioned her through. Wind whisked through her hair, shoving more loose strands across her face as she stepped onto the roof. Roy moved behind her and the door clanked closed.

Storm clouds again hovered on the horizon, over the waters of the Pacific. Her sweater pressed against her body from the wind and she turned her face away. There, to her right, lay a small, compact helicopter on its side.

If he could right it, it had room for two people.

Her and Roy.

Oh, hell no.

"Shit." Roy limped away from her, across the rooftop in the direction of the helicopter.

She spun towards the door, grabbed the outside lever and shoved it downward to open it. A strong arm wrapped around her waist, hauled her off the ground.

"No." She beat her fists against the door, against the arm at her waist. Kicked backwards. "Let me go."

"Never." He shook her once, hard, then smacked the side of her face with his palm.

With a curse, he shoved her aside. "I warned you. I will hurt you if you force me to."

She stumbled backwards, away from him, and fell. Slightly dazed, her movements slow, she forced herself into a half sitting, half kneeling position. With a hand pressed to her stinging cheek, she lifted her gaze to meet his. "You're choice, not mine."

"Wrong." He squatted in front of her, tilted his head slightly to the side before he touched her hair. He stroked the length of a long strand then ran the tip of his index finger down her other cheek. "You will never get away from me, Calea. Never."

GAVIN STOOD, BACK to the Hummer with his hands splayed at his waist, in the hotel's parking structure. Completely still, he ignored the rush of mid-morning wind that brought the heavy scent of coming rain. Ignored the burn of his now bandaged left arm.

First aid kit in the rear of the Hummer. Enough for now, until Calea was safe.

After numerous, unobtrusive scans, he still didn't believe what his senses told him, that he was alone here at the hotel. Not another living person for miles.

He hadn't heard the helicopter, any helicopter, and he'd listened for one on the way here. If that bird had been on this roof, it was still there. He just had to get to the copter without Hoffman sensing his presence. And before they took off.

Piece of cake.

Bad things happen when one of us says that. Calea's words echoed.

Not this time, sweetheart. *I'm coming for you. I won't stop until I find you.*

Convinced Hoffman had, somehow, been tracking Calea all along, Gavin headed toward the stairwell. Careful being the word of the hour, he couldn't misjudge the other man. Not again.

At each level, his hands cupped around the butt of his weapon, he paused to expand his senses.

Maybe he was alone, and maybe he wasn't.

Instinct warred with urgency.

He wouldn't be doing anyone a favor if he got himself shot again.

At the door to the roof he still hadn't found a trace of anyone else in the building. Cautious, he eased open the door and stepped onto the roof.

To the right the helicopter lay on its side. One landing skid in the air.

Well. Gavin's mouth lifted in a half smile. Hoffman wouldn't be escaping that way.

Definite plus. But where the hell were they? What would Hoffman's next plan entail?

Hide.

Until the bridge was repaired and access to the outside world was restored.

As he and Calea had tried to do yesterday.

Question was, here or elsewhere. And where was elsewhere?

On the left, a few feet away, was another door, this one with a regular doorknob rather than a handle. Gavin stood in front of the door with his hand flat against it, fingers spread wide. With nothing out of the ordinary pinging his senses, he tried the knob and the door swung inward.

An almost empty storage shed with another window washing rig.

Chains in a tangled mess, cut sections of rope.

He angled his head, scanned the roof line.

There, across the roof on the ocean side of the building, he spied one end of a rope tied to a metal pipe extruding from the cement. The other end of the rope disappeared over the edge.

He'd bet money their tenth floor room was right there. That Hoffman had used that rope to scale down one floor and swing into their room.

Which opened up more possibilities.

Gavin eased the shed door closed. Stared at the helicopter.

From the way the copter lay, its radio would be of no use. Aimed downward, the range would be nonexistent.

No help there.

What he needed was to find Calea.

With a last glance at the helicopter, he moved to stand in front of the stairwell door. On an uneasy inward breath, he again expanded his senses, stretched them outward.

Calea?

Again nothing.

Wait.

Something.

He wasn't one of Garrett's Psi agents, wasn't a hunter. But he'd been around enough of them, in the field, to have a sense of how they worked. And now, like out in that bramble of vines, that aberration, that little inkling of something off, teased the edges of his mind.

There, but not there, pulling at him.

Something not right.

Chapter Twelve

CALEA LEANED HER head against the back of the couch and held the ice, wrapped in a damp towel, to her swollen cheek. At least Roy had untied her.

He now sat on the perfectly made, king-sized bed with his legs stretched out in front of him and his back against the headboard. Earlier, he'd left for a short time then came back with more black clothes and a manila file folder thick with papers. That folder he'd tossed on one of the tables before he'd showered and tended his gunshot wound.

Now, at this moment, he didn't seem the slightest bit interested in her and she was grateful for that. No, right now he seemed lost in his own head, barely aware of her presence. She didn't see that as a bad thing.

"Dunbar is a nuisance."

"Excuse me?" She kept her voice low, with barely any infliction.

A deep breath expanded Roy's chest before he let it go. "Exterminating him would be so much simpler if it weren't for you."

"He's here?" She straightened, gripped the damp towel between her hands and pressed what was left of the ice cubes together. She pushed her senses outward, met Roy's wall. *Dammit.*

"Stop testing me, Calea." Roy levelled that flat gaze at her.

"You said you wouldn't shoot him again." *To hell with moderating my tone.* She sat the towel on the coffee table in front of her.

"Did I?"

"Yes."

"I should have killed him."

A sudden lump, the size of a grapefruit, expanded in her chest. Squeezed out all of her air. *Breathe.* "Why didn't you?"

"If I had, I was pretty sure you wouldn't have been willing to help me."

I'm still not willing. "I don't have any idea how I'm supposed to help you."

"Doesn't matter. Turns out you don't have to cooperate. Makes it all so much simpler."

"What are you talking about?"

"Killing Dunbar."

"Roy —"

"His persistence is pissing me off. But, I told you I wouldn't shoot him, so I won't. For you, I'll keep my word. Instead, I'll use a knife." His mouth lifted in a slight smile. "So much more satisfying that way."

Oh, God. That lump filled her chest cavity. "Where is he now?"

"On the roof."

"How do you know that?" *Gavin's so close. How do I warn him?*

Roy stood, adjusted the hem of the snug T-shirt he wore then pulled on one of the button down shirts he'd come back with, this one as black as his other clothes. He let it hang open, all the while watching her. "Come here."

"Like hell."

"If you don't do as I say, you'll find out what hell's all about."

She pushed herself up from the couch, shook her head.

"Quit fighting me, Calea." He moved a few feet closer.

"I don't know *how* to stop fighting." Her heart pounded hard against the lump in her chest. She scurried behind the wing-backed chair and braced her hands on the top. Her only defense was keeping him away from her. That and the lamp on the table between the chair and the couch.

"Then I'll have to teach you." Although he hadn't moved, his ominous intent swelled. Swamped her.

"No."

One side of his mouth lifted. His eyes, no longer flat, burned with a sudden inner intensity. "You belong to me, Calea Fontaine. Only me. Forever."

Obsessed. Insane.

She shook her head. Keep him talking. "How do you —"

"Know your real last name, *Callie?*"

"Yes." Her fingers dug into the chair's material. "You work for Milford."

"Not any more. Not since I figured out *why* he wanted you."

"And what is that reason? Why would he want me? Why would that make any difference to you?" She pressed her lips together. This man in front of her had killed Tommy. Her student. "You *are* the one who attacked me all those months ago."

"Son of a bitch." Roy, his head lifted and his face suddenly pale, stood motionless for several heartbeats. Then he fisted both hands. His nostrils flared as his breathing quickened. "No."

Gavin? She stretched her senses, reached for him.

There. *Gavin.*

A door slammed in her mind, vibrating down to her toes, severing the tenuous link she'd forged with Gavin.

"No." Roy's gaze, wild around the edges, bored into her. "You belong to me."

She squeezed the chair. Calculated how quick she could grab the lamp to smash it across his skull.

"Touch me."

She shook her head.

In one move he shoved the chair to the side and grabbed both her wrists. "I said, touch me, Calea."

"I won't." Her hands balled tight, she struggled to twist away from him.

"When I tell you to touch me, you will." He yanked her closer, forced her fists open to press both her palms to his cheeks.

His skin, clammy and cold to hers, warmed under her hands. Her continued struggles ignored, he closed his eyes and lowered his forehead to hers. She pulled back, reared to knee him in the groin, but he yanked her flush again. He let go of one of her hands to press her body to his.

With her free hand, she clawed at his cheek and neck.

Drew blood.

She reached to scratch him again, but he clamped a hand over her wrist then twisted it behind her back, arching her closer to him. The hand he still held to his other cheek he moved to his mouth. With his eyes open and his gaze strikingly clear and locked on hers, he pressed his lips to her palm.

"No." She yanked on her hand, fought to pull away from him.

Suddenly free, she fell against the side of the chair but didn't pause as she scrambled backwards to right the chair and situate it between them again.

Roy just stood there, watching her, a slight smile playing over his lips.

In his eyes.

With those few feet separating her from him, she rubbed her sore wrists. "You're different than you were a few moments ago. What does my touch do to you?"

The edges of his mouth quirked. "Centers me."

Shit. "How?"

He shrugged both shoulders, shook his head. "All I know is that it does."

"And that's why Milford wanted me?" She searched Roy's face. His skin, no longer pale, held the tan of a man who'd spent a lot of time outdoors. Before now, she would have said he hardly went outside. That he had the pale skin of a man who'd rarely enjoyed the sunshine. "Are you sick?"

"Not in a normal sense."

"You followed me to Oregon?"

"Hardly, considering I was here first."

"But —"

"Your student told me of this place. That this is where you come to recharge."

"Tommy." A chill scudded down her spine. She blinked back sudden tears and gripped the back of the chair. Shook her head. "You killed him."

"You haven't established that I've actually killed anyone yet."

"But you have." Her hands fisted. "I can see it inside you."

He shrugged one shoulder.

"And Tommy's one of those you've murdered."

His lips thinned. Something flickered inside those dark eyes.

So he didn't like being called out. "And John, the manager here? His chef?"

Roy's chin jerked a small, almost immeasurable amount.

They were also gone. "Why?"

But not Gavin. Not yet. *How do I keep that from happening?*

Roy held her gaze for one long, drawn out moment before he spun on his heel, grabbed the manila file folder from the table where it sat and swung back to shove the folder towards her.

Hesitant, her gaze locked on his and, sure whatever was in that folder would change things yet again, she leaned forward to gingerly take the folder. She held it in front of her between both hands. "What's in here?"

"You wanted answers."

On the tenth floor, at the door to the concierge, Gavin stood with his legs braced apart. With his senses wide open he tested the hallway area and the rooms beyond.

Nothing.

No Calea. No aberration.

He'd sworn, several times, he'd caught the feel of her. A quick spark of her presence, of her energy. There, then gone.

And he'd sworn it had come from the tenth floor.

That earlier flash he'd picked up of the aberration was also gone. As if it had never existed.

Made him want to question if it *had* existed.

But that was a fool's query. He knew what he'd felt. Knew what the damn thing felt like. And now he was going to *hunt* the bastard down.

Artificially Enhanced Abilities.

Those three words, from the first page of the report Roy had shoved at her a few minutes ago, circled in a downward spiral through Calea's mind. From behind the chair she kept between her and Roy, she glanced towards where he now sat sprawled on the couch several feet away.

All relaxed. The foot of his hurt leg resting on the coffee table and one arm tucked behind his head, those eyes half closed, masking that feral look she knew lurked there. Apparently not a care in the world.

"You were part of an experiment?" She rubbed her forehead. "To what end?"

The edge of his mouth quirked. "Finish reading the report."

She shook her head. None of this made any kind of rational sense.

He kept that half hooded gaze locked on her.

Fine. She glanced at the papers in her hand then at him. "According to this, you started out with decent hunter capabilities, excellent shielding and an innate ability to stay under the radar."

One slow nod.

"And when they injected you with this *mystery* substance, all those aptitudes magnified in proportion." She shook her head again. "Roy, this reads like science fiction."

And again the quirk at the edge of his mouth.

"Who are *they* and what is this mysterious substance?"

"A precursor for a brand new drug out of Europe." Roy shrugged a shoulder. "From some special tree found only in one tiny country."

"All of this was done to you with a new drug?"

"Not the drug itself. The precursor."

"You haven't said *who*. Milford is behind this? Is he implicated anywhere in here?" She flipped through several pages.

Roy stretched his other leg out and crossed his hurt leg over the other at the ankles. "No, Milford's not mentioned anywhere in there. I didn't show you that to nail him."

"Then why?"

"For you to understand. What they did to me. What I'm now capable of doing. Why I need to keep you."

"I'm not a pet."

Both sides of his mouth lifted in an icy semblance of a smile. "Here, kitty, kitty."

Her gaze, locked on him, narrowed.

That almost smile disappeared. "Keep reading."

"What am I looking for?"

"Do you ever just do what you're damn well told to do?"

"No. Do you?"

"Page four. Half way down."

She held his hooded gaze for a half second longer then glanced to the ceiling before flipping the report to page four.

Extraordinary results: Skill at blending into environment magnified. Now excels at camouflage, becoming nearly invisible. Hunting abilities / Warrior instincts heightened ten-fold.

High tolerance for pain.

Periods of instability.

Calea swallowed. That couldn't be good. "Are you still taking this precursor?"

He shook his head.

That was something, at least. "Have the effects faded at all?"

"No. And it isn't believed they will. The way it was explained to me, it's like they flipped a switch and it's now permanent."

Wonderful.

"Keep reading."

She flicked a glare his way, but then continued to read. The last sentence in the next paragraph jumped out at her.

Recommendation: A controller, versed in grounding, is a necessity.

"You think I'm this controller?"

"I know you are."

"Why?"

"Tommy."

Back to her student. "What does he have to do with anything? He was a good kid. He had a bit of trouble controlling himself, but that was no reason to kill him."

Controlling.

She wet her lips. Shook her head. "I wasn't his controller. I was simply his teacher."

"According to him, you were much more than that. You quieted the monsters in his mind."

"No. He didn't have monsters."

A sly smile crossed Roy's mouth. "We all have monsters, Calea."

Her legs trembled. Lord, she wanted to sit down. To pull her knees to her chest, bury her head in her hands. Will this all away. She shook her head again. "Yours must be doozies."

"You have no idea."

"I can't help you any more than I helped Tommy." She tossed the report onto the seat of the chair she kept between her and Roy. "He had a hard time accepting any kind of responsibility for himself. Maybe he projected this *quieting* ability to me, but he was wrong. I'm not any kind of controller. I'm a teacher."

"Then why did Milford send Tommy with me to retrieve you? Why was Tommy so excited to see you? And why is Milford so sure you can help me?"

"Is? You're in touch with Milford?"

"He thinks I'm dead. I made sure of that."

"When you killed Tommy."

"This is getting tedious. You want to know *how* I know you're what I *need*?" He laced his fingers together over his stomach. "You touch me and I can *think* again. The monsters go away. My mind clears."

"I can't ground you."

He slammed a fist on the arm of the couch, so fast she hadn't seen him move. "You're not paying attention, Calea."

"You're not being rational."

"Oh, but I am. And in order to remain so, I *need* you to touch me when I tell you to do so. To not argue with me. To be the controller I have to have."

"What if I get away, if I escape? Then what happens to you?"

"I will go completely insane." His mouth widened into a nasty smile. His eyes took on a dark inner glow. "I doubt you'd like to be responsible for the consequences of that happening."

Chapter Thirteen

G AVIN, HIS GUN pointed up and his back against the wall opposite the tenth floor elevators, shoved his senses outward once more.

Testing.

Better to be sure than sorry.

Nothing. He might be the only person in this building. That's what his senses told him. But he didn't believe that. Didn't trust that.

Time to move.

Kill.

Gavin stilled.

Intent. Pure and unadorned. And not his.

Hoffman's?

Gavin focused.

Heat, thick with contempt, brushed over his skin. Prickled. Radiated an instant burning pain.

Shields, born of caution and adrenaline, snapped into place.

Shit. Too late to conceal his presence.

Gavin ran a finger under his collar, pulled at the material. Damn hallway was closing in, making it hard to breathe. So Hoffman knew he was here and intended to kill him this time.

Right.

Gavin eased the stairwell door open then retreated back up the stairs. No need to be an easy target.

Once back on the roof, with his shields locked down in place close to his body, a dull itch coating his skin and his lungs tight, he hunkered down against the helicopter. He had a direct view of the stairwell door.

Time to regroup.

Hoffman might, somehow, be able to make himself, and Calea, invisible, but going through solid objects, like the damn door to the roof, was too much to swallow. Gavin hoped. The bastard was close. Knew Gavin had been in the stairwell on the tenth floor.

But that's all the man knew.

A sudden gust of wind blew, swirled fast across the roof to scatter pieces of debris here and there and plaster his shirt against him. That gust also brought the scent of ocean and the coming storm.

Gavin rechecked his weapon.

Whatever the hell Hoffman was, able to hide in plain sight, both on the physical level *and* in the psychic arena, went beyond anything he'd seen before now.

And he'd seen some weird shit working with Garrett and his teams.

So what now?

Hoffman was close. And that had to mean Calea was also near.

Gavin pulled at his collar.

Damn shields.

How could he get down into the hotel itself without Hoffman knowing? Not down the stairs. The man would be looking for him, and with that damn ability to go invisible, Gavin might not sense him until too late.

Can't have that.

Scale down the side? Which floor?

Tenth. There was already a room with the windows out, courtesy of Hoffman's visit last evening. They wouldn't be in there, not when so many other rooms would be much more comfortable.

Gavin's stomach clenched.

If Hoffman had done *anything* to her, he was going to kill the man himself.

No hesitation.

The rope was already tied off. Already marked the spot.

All he had to do was head over the side. Drop into the room. Keep his presence concealed.

Piece of cake.

The corners of his mouth lifted. *I'm coming, sweetheart.*

CALEA LEANED FORWARD in her chair and sat the file folder on the coffee table. Roy stood a few feet away, hands on his hips and half angled toward her with his gaze locked on something outside the window.

Late morning, but it might as well be approaching dusk, the clouds were so thick and dark. Wind battered the window with debris full of leaves and twigs broken off the trees.

Gavin was out there, somewhere, looking for her, while Roy planned some kind of ambush.

Had she ever felt so damn helpless?

"Where the hell is he?" Roy's hands fisted at his hips. "Where did he go?"

Something akin to hope flickered in her chest. "You don't know?"

His gaze, dark and again flat, locked on her. "I will."

She swallowed once as he stared back out the window. "Maybe Ben, my boss, can help you. Maybe he can figure out a way to reverse the effects."

"I know who Ben Garrett is, but I have no desire to reverse anything. I have you, now."

"Dammit, Roy. What you're doing is kidnapping. Holding me against my will."

That side of his mouth lifted, but he didn't glance back at her. "I'm well aware of what I'm doing."

"And you don't care? Am I nothing more than a means to an end? Stupid questions. What's a little kidnapping compared to murdering how many people?"

"One more before the day is over."

"What?" *Not Gavin.*

"He's dropped off the radar." Roy, his eyes narrowed, lifted his head. "I had him, but that was nearly twenty minutes ago. He's tenacious. I doubt he's left the building. Not without you. That's one thing we have in common."

She held her breath.

Roy aimed his dark gaze at her. "I wouldn't have thought him good enough to completely shield himself.

He didn't seem to have that level of ability. To be able to hide his presence so completely."

Gavin. Yesterday she'd have agreed. But yesterday she didn't understand Gavin's reasons for avoiding shields. His mother and her claustrophobic overprotectiveness. Avoiding wasn't nearly the same thing as not having the ability.

Shielding wasn't the same thing as being able to go invisible, either. And *that* was something Gavin couldn't do, couldn't combat.

"Without a sense of his shields, he will be harder to track." Roy's voice held a measure of curiosity. Almost of intrigue.

That couldn't be good. *Wait a minute.* "You sense shields?"

"How do you think I found *you* this morning, so easily?"

"But –"

"Shields are little more than a bending of reality. A 'don't see me' shroud of safety that's nothing more than an illusion of unrealistic security. A trick of the light, a slight of the hand. For the practitioner and the hunter. *If* that hunter believes it."

"And you don't."

"Hardly. It took longer than I'd anticipated, but now I know what your shield feels like. Therefore, as a hunter, I can find you." He turned his head, met her gaze. "I will *always* be able to find you."

GAVIN PULLED ON the knot tying the rope to the length of pipe protruding from the roof.

Secure.

He tightened his fingers around the material. This rope matched the cut pieces in the shed where the rigging lay, so this was how Hoffman had scaled down the side of the hotel yesterday.

How the man had managed to break the window, Gavin wasn't sure, but right now *that* room was where he was headed.

He rotated his head, aware of each bone cracking creak. Damn shields, locked in place, pressed on him from every damn direction.

Not even the wind lashing at him or the rain soaking his clothes weighed as heavy.

But he had no choice. Shield or let Hoffman know his location.

One last look over the edge and Gavin nodded.

Now or never.

With his weapon at the small of his back and the rope wrapped around the elbow of his uninjured arm, secured in both hands, he eased himself over the side. Found purchase against the side of the building with his feet.

Thank God for tennis shoes.

Lightning flashed somewhere close, towards the south. The scent of ozone lingered.

All right. From this vantage, not quite dangling, the broken window, with pieces of glass scattered along the sill, stood open like a mouth full of jagged teeth.

The rope bit into his palms as he tightened his grip. He lowered himself a few more feet, kicked at the window to break more of the glass then braced his feet on the outside sill.

On an inward breath, he bent his knees, getting closer to the window. Outward breath, he shoved himself backwards, pulled his knees up then thrust his legs forward to launch himself through the window.

Letting go of the rope, he twisted and landed in the room, one knee down, one knee up and both hands flat on the floor. His head came up, hand went to his back and fingers gripped the butt of his gun as he quickly scanned the room.

Empty.

All around him shattered fragments of glass lay in a room tossed as thoroughly and as wrecked as his own hotel room had been yesterday morning.

For the moment, he left his weapon at the small of his back and pushed himself to stand. He wiped his hands gingerly over his thighs, careful of any glass shards. Lucky he didn't have any stuck in his palms.

So far, so good.

Now what?

Thick drapes, although heavy with moisture, moved with the wind funneled in through the window. The bedding of the king-size bed, where less than twenty-four hours ago he and Calea had made love, lay in a heap against the far wall while the mattress itself was half skewed off the box springs with gaping holes slashed through the top.

His jaw twitched. Nostrils flared.

He'd burn that bastard in hell if he hurt Calea.

Focus, Dunbar. Stuff the reaction for now.

There had to be some way to track that son of a bitch.

Mentally he started to reach for Calea.

No.

That might have been how Hoffman had found him before. Granted, he might have found him simply because his shielding had sucked.

Shit. So many unknowns.

Gavin eased another layer of protective energy into the damn thing.

Main objective. Find Calea. Then drop his shields and let her take over the mental barrier business. She was so much better at it, and maybe, somehow, he'd learn to tolerate her shields.

But right now, no reaching for or mentally searching for Calea.

What then?

The aberration.

He moved towards the hotel room door, stepping over pieces of what might have been a coffee table and a broken lamp. Fine, white feathers, probably from the down pillows that had once sat against the headboard, lay strewn across the carpet.

At the door he stopped, stood with his arms at his side, his palms forward.

He'd seen hunters stand this way. Hadn't thought much about it before now. But, shit, if the pose helped channel whatever the hell they were looking for, he'd try it.

His eyes closed, quieting his mind, he mentally skimmed the area just outside the door.

Nothing.

He evened his breathing then on an exhale pushed his senses further out.

Then again.

And again.

There.

With his eyes still closed he frowned.

Something, to the left, down the hallway.

What the hell was that?

Not the aberration. Not the same. Different. But –

The same. At the center.

Hoffman?

If what Gavin sensed earlier had been Hoffman concealing himself in some kind of cloak of invisibility, didn't it stand to reason that, at the center, Hoffman's energy would have the same feel to it?

And if he wasn't cloaking himself, he'd be easier to find.

Theoretically.

Gavin opened his eyes, shoved an additional spurt of energy into his own shields then pulled his weapon and checked the peephole. Empty. He eased the door open and checked the perimeter.

Still empty.

His gun leading, he stepped into the hallway.

Nothing. No one.

He turned to the left. Followed the thread as it strengthened. Not wanting to draw attention to himself, he eased back on his scan and again amped up the level of his shields, adding another layer. No sense announcing his presence.

Four doors down from the one he'd entered through the window, the thread pulsed. Almost like a heartbeat.

This was the spot.

CALEA SWALLOWED HARD against the bile rising in her throat. She keep her gaze on Roy as he paced the length of the room. Every few feet he stopped, lifted his head as his gaze went out of focus.

Psychically searching for Gavin.

Roy *couldn't* find him. That much was obvious.

Had Gavin left? Gone for reinforcements?

He wouldn't have left her here, alone with Roy. *Stupid.* How could he have any freaking idea where she was? Of where Roy was holding her?

But Gavin was working to find her. To save her. That's who he was, what he did. Maybe he was shielding himself. The man who hated shields. Lord, she hoped so. But she couldn't reach out. If Roy didn't block her, he'd use her to lure Gavin in. She couldn't allow that to happen.

Couldn't pull Gavin in to meet his death.

She hunched her shoulders forward and continued to watch Roy.

After several trips back and forth across the room he stopped a few feet from her, his hands fisted at his hips and his legs shoulder width apart. "Come here."

She swallowed again but shook her head.

"I said, come here."

Her gaze locked on his, she again shook her head.

Something flashed through his dark eyes, something harsh and a bit wild. "Calea. Don't test me."

She pulled her legs up so that her bare feet rested on the edge of the chair and her knees were at her chest.

"Dammit." He lunged forward.

With everything she had, she kicked out. Her right foot connected with his left knee. He screamed, the bellow rending the air, and he went down to the floor beside her. She scrambled backwards and upwards, to her full height. Then she leapt over him.

Got to get away.

Less than three feet from the door it burst open. Gavin surged inside.

Her breath caught in her chest, expanded. Sudden warm moisture filled her eyes. *Oh, Lord. Gavin.* She flung herself at him. "Turn. Go. Run."

Without missing a beat, he wrapped an arm around her waist, pivoted and shoved her in front of him and out of the door. He slammed it behind him and pulled her down the hallway to where another door stood open.

Once inside the other room, he slammed that door shut and locked it. He slid his weapon under his waistband at his back then yanked her into his arms.

His mouth on hers. Hot. Demanding. Hard.

Then gone.

"We have to get out of here." He set her away from him but ran both hands over her shoulders, down her arms, then up to grip her shoulders through the material of her sweater. His gaze darkened as he searched her face then ran the back of his fingers lightly over the edge of the bruise on her cheek. "Son of a bitch."

"I'm okay." *Now.*

Gavin's shields, since Roy couldn't read them, might hide her also. *If* Gavin continued to touch her maybe that would keep her from being discovered.

Protect them both.

If she could make him understand.

"Gavin —" Her hands shook as, careful of her sore cheek, she pressed them over his.

And dropped what little shielding she still had. Completely.

Naked. Vulnerable. Lord, she hated this sensation. But she couldn't jeopardize them. Couldn't be the reason they were found again.

"What the hell, Calea?" Gavin frowned. "Come on, sunshine, snap those shields back in place and we'll blow this joint."

"I c-c-can't." Damn this stupid trembling. *Maintain.* Gavin's shields were still there. They still encompassed her. Not completely naked. She had to make him understand.

Had to trust.

He took both her hands, pressed them together between his. Warmth seeped into skin she hadn't realized was chilled. He bent forward so his troubled gaze met hers. "Why can't you? What's happened?"

"Roy *reads* my shields." She took a deep breath. "That's how he tracks us. Tracks me. Through them."

"That's not –" Gavin frowned as he gently squeezed her fingers. "How do we hide from him?"

"He can't read *yours*." *Please understand.* "You hid from him. He couldn't find you. You were on the roof and then gone."

Gavin, his face tight, nodded once.

"You couldn't see *me* when he did his invisible thing. Because he was holding me. Right now, with your hands on me, I can feel your shields surrounding us both. *Maybe*, if you set the intent, deliberately stretch your shields around me while you're touching me, you can do something similar."

"I'm not any good at this, Calea." Doubt edged the seriousness of his expression.

"But you've managed to block him so far. And if he was able to read *me* within your shields, he'd already be in here. So you must be doing something right." She shivered. "Just don't let go of me."

He nodded again. Narrowed his gaze.

The undercurrent of the air around them rippled. Settled. Her breath caught then her lungs expanded. He'd done it, shields more secured around their bodies.

Home.

Oh, goodness. She'd never *felt* his shields before. He still held her hands, but it was as if his arms encircled her, pressed her to his body.

Protected. Sheltered.

Safe.

Tension in her shoulders eased. Melted.

Gavin.

He twisted his head, side to side.

Obviously not any more comfortable inside his own shields than inside anyone else's.

"Just until he's caught." She whispered the words but caught the short, quick jerk of his chin.

"Let's go."

"Where to?" She turned her hands, gripped his as she took one step back from him before he scooped her up, his good arm under her legs and the other around her waist. "What are you doing?"

"Glass on the floor."

"You're injured."

"I'm fine."

"Maybe you are, but I have shoes somewhere in here."

"Had. Hoffman destroyed everything that was left."

"Oh." She'd been too focused on Gavin, on his shields and making him understand. With a quick look around, dismay clenched her stomach tight.

Destroy was an understatement. Utter destruction.

Material from the couch lay strewn across the room in tattered strands, tangled with remnants of one of the inner curtains and chucks of wood that might once have been the couch's frame.

Or the bed's.

She couldn't tell.

Shredded fabric lay on top of the scattered mess.

Even the wall hangings and overhead lights had been yanked down and thrashed.

So much violence.

She wrapped her arms around Gavin's neck and pressed her forehead to his cheek. "Thank you for being there when you were."

He angled his head. Kissed her forehead. "That's my job, sweetheart."

Right. Job. Protect her. Wasn't that why he was here? Why he'd come in the first place?

Keep her safe. Get her back behind the Institute's walls.

Where none of this would have happened if she'd stayed put.

But it had and she needed to make sure Gavin understood the extent of what they were up against. He had a plan. But he didn't have all the facts.

She straightened as he headed deeper into the room. Glass crunched underneath his feet.

"That invisibility thing of Roy's, Gavin, is just part of what he can do." She bit the inside of her bottom lip. How to explain in simple terms, considering they didn't have the time to go into any kind of depth? "All of his senses, his abilities, are heightened to the nth degree."

"I got that. Null he isn't."

Damp air, colder here closer to the gaping hole in the outside wall, swirled in through the broken windows to press against her body and add to the chill skittering over her entire body.

"Not even close." Her toes curled against the cold, she burrowed into Gavin, against his chest. "He's been experimented on. Altered. He showed me his file. Even the doctors have no idea what he can do, how far his abilities have expanded. He's off their charts. He's no longer measurable."

"What else did the doctors say?" The low rumble of Gavin's voice settled a small fraction of the gnawing in her stomach.

Her eyes closed, she rubbed her cheek over the soft material of his shirt. "That he'd gotten to a point where he was uncontrollable. A danger to everyone around him. They ended up recommending he be taken out. Killed."

Chapter Fourteen

*D*AMN STRAIGHT.

Take the bastard out.

Gavin wrapped his arms around Calea, held her loose against him, and wrestled with the foreign sensation of his shields pressed outwards and against him at the same time. He sucked in a lungful of the damp, cold air blowing in through the broken window.

Less than fifteen minutes since he'd tracked the aberration to that particular room and kicked the door in to find Calea barreling straight towards him. Now the two of them stood in the same room they'd hidden in yesterday.

With *him* concealing their presence this time.

Like holding spun sugar in his arms, he stroked her back while he rubbed his cheek lightly over her hair. Her clothes weren't torn. Beyond the bruise, she seemed all right.

Physically.

But she was shaken. Traumatized.

What the hell had the man done to her?

Right now, taking Hoffman out was number one on Gavin's list.

But how the hell was he going to accomplish that if he couldn't let go of Calea? If he had to be physically connected, touching her, to keep her safe inside his shields?

Irony at its finest.

His shields protecting someone else.

"Now what do we do?" Her sigh feathered his skin, warmed his neck. "Wait?"

He shifted, tightening his hold on her.

She leaned away and searched his gaze. "Even if your arm really is *fine*, you can't stand here holding me."

He cocked an eyebrow, made her smile. Then he pressed his lips to her temple. "And we can't stay in here. I'd say it's only a short amount of time before Hoffman checks this room."

"So sitting tight and waiting is out of the question." She pulled the edge of her bottom lip between her teeth.

Frustration festered in his gut. He couldn't leave her vulnerable.

Shit. He'd spent his life running from other people's shields. Had refused to learn *how* to use his own efficiently, had refused to use them *period*.

And now, if he didn't use them adeptly, the woman he loved would be in imminent danger.

Irony.

He twisted to lean against the wall next to the window then slid down to squat on his heels, Calea cradled in his lap. "Hold on."

Resting her legs on his, he reached behind to pull his weapon out.

No sense being any more unprepared.

"Gavin? You can't go after him, alone." Her eyes full of worry, she ran the tip of her index finger down his cheek. Tingles followed the path. "Unless you want me to bait him. I could do that. We could ambush him."

"Like hell." And that was the crux. There was no way he'd willingly risk her safety. He held her gaze. Nodded once. "We stay together. We can head to the roof. The helicopter is there. Not flyable, but we can tuck in behind it. Wait."

"How do we get there?" She flicked that worried gaze towards the door. "He could be anywhere, even right outside that door, and we wouldn't see him."

He'd know. He doubted he'd ever be able to shake the sense of that aberration, but precaution wasn't a bad thing. "We go up. By rope. The way I came in."

Her eyes widened. "Through the window?"

"Come on, sweetheart." He kissed the tip of her nose. "Piece of cake."

"Right." She rolled her eyes. "Do I cuss you out now or later?"

"How about once we're on the roof?"

"Gavin —"

"When I stand, wrap your legs around my waist and your arms around my neck." This would be so much easier if they didn't have to stay in contact, but it was what it was and they'd make it. Together. "At the window, once I have the rope, grab it. You'll pull yourself up, but I'll be right against you. My hand just above yours. In constant touch."

This would work. In spite of his injury, they could make this work. Thank God she had that rock climbing wall back at the Institute. He'd stood in the gym doorway, watched her work with her students. Knew she had the basics down. They could do this.

"Got it?"

On a deep breath she nodded.

He pushed himself to a standing position and she wrapped herself around him.

Oh for this not being such a critical situation.

He stole a quick kiss. For luck.

Her sudden intake of breath headed straight for his groin.

Okay, then.

"Let's go." He shoved his weapon back behind his back, tucked into his waistband. With her wrapped around him, he seized the dangling rope and eased to lean backwards out the window. At least the rain had tapered off. "Grab hold."

She eased her grip on his neck, twisted slightly to hook the rope. Her gaze caught his and a tremulous smile brightened her face. "Let's do this thing."

Now or never.

He leaned back further to give her room to maneuver. With the rope wrapped around her elbow and wrist, she angled her back to him and pulled both legs up to brace her bare feet against the wet outside wall. Once both her hands were on the rope, he gripped it, hands just above hers but touching.

Outside, with Calea's bare feet steadied on the wall to the right of the window, he levered himself up on the far right of the ledge, rope in his hands, and his body cupping hers.

The key would be to stay in constant contact at some point between their bodies.

And his shields intact.

Damp wind buffeted him, pierced through his clothes.

Ignore.

He eased his hands up the rope and she followed with hers then he stabilized his feet against the wall and she shimmied another foot upwards. With his chest pressed to her back, he moved his hands again and they repeated the process.

A foot at a time, each movement slow and deliberate.

Slow, painful progress.

Until they reached the edge of the roof.

They were nearly golden. Unless Hoffman waited on the other side of the ledge.

Gavin, ignoring the burn of his wound, stretched his senses out, searching for that aberration. For the core essence of the bastard. For anything out of place.

Nothing.

Gavin and Calea could be the only two people around. For miles.

That sensation bothered him more than anything else.

Where the hell was Hoffman?

"Hold on here." Gavin rubbed his cheek, light, over her hair. "Let me do a quick visual scan."

She nodded, wrapped the rope an extra time around her elbow and wrist then bent her knees, curling her body closer to the wall and giving him room to straighten, to take a look over the edge, and stay in contact with her.

Again nothing.

No one. Nobody.

No Hoffman.

"Clear." Gavin glanced down, met Calea's upward gaze. Now came the tricky part. Getting onto the roof. "Ease yourself up a bit higher, so that you're almost flush with the wall. I'm going to boost you up and over the ledge. Once there, it'll be up to you to keep contact while I pull myself over. Ready?"

She nodded, breathed deep then in slow increments she straightened until her legs pressed against his, her back to his chest. They both bent their knees, walking their feet another foot up the wall. He secured the rope around one wrist and let go with the other hand to cup her thighs and lift.

With the extra help from him, she pulled herself up to the edge. He wrapped his hand around her bare foot, her skin ice cold to his touch, and leveraged her higher. She gripped the lip of the roofline and let go of the rope.

"Push." She took a deep breath, and hauled her upper body onto the roof. Then, with his free hand on her foot, she levered herself the rest of the way, pulling her knees underneath to rest on the roof.

After a short moment, with Gavin's fingers still wrapped lightly around one foot, she twisted and sat with her legs dangling over the lip, her heels against the wall to the right of the rope.

She leaned forward to grip his forearm. "Your turn."

"Right." He let go of her foot, trusting her to maintain contact. He could wish all he wanted, but the fact remained he had no idea how to encompass her within his shields without that contact.

Something he'd remedy once they were out of this mess.

Along with several other issues.

Being bigger and more active than Calea, he made short work of getting over the lip and onto the roof. Once there, he pulled the rope up behind him then squatted on one heel with his other foot flat on the roof. She sat, legs over the edge, her hand still gripped on his arm.

He lay his palm on her hand and she rotated hers so their palms met. Then she linked their fingers. Somewhere deep in his chest the fire with her name all over it blazed a bit warmer.

His gaze locked on hers. The corner of his mouth lifted in a half grin.

They'd made it this far.

"Ready, sweetheart?" He tugged on her hand.

She answered with a grin of her own and, their fingers still linked, scrambled to stand when he did. "As I'll ever be."

"Want me to carry you?"

"Please." Sarcasm, as only Calea could manage, dripped from the word. She scanned the area, her gaze sweeping over the expanse of wet concrete with its puddles of rainwater and strewn fall leaves from the previous storms. "I got this."

Nothing to really damage those pretty feet of hers.

"Let's do it." He pulled his weapon then rechecked for the aberration.

Not there.

Fingers entwined, they sprinted across the roof towards the small, squat helicopter that lay as it had been, on its side, with one door wrenched open and half off its hinges. The bulbous, clear nose reflected back the heaviness of the low hanging clouds while the brininess of the ocean air mixed in the breeze. Not much longer before the rain would be pounding them again.

Gun in hand, Gavin pulled Calea around the nose, skimming the top of the craft to brace themselves along the main rotor mast between the cabin and the rotors. Not a lot of protection here, the helicopter was small and that damn nose was clear and see through. But it was something physical between them and the stairwell door.

Beyond the rotors, only a few feet stretched to the eastern edge of the roof. Unless Hoffman scaled that wall, they were secure on that front. That left only the stairwell for vulnerability.

All said, this had been easy. Too easy.

He didn't trust easy.

"Keep your hand on my arm." For the hundredth time, he tested the perimeter of his shields, scanned for the aberration. All as it should be. Hell, he didn't trust that, either.

"Gavin." Her fingers squeezed his wrist.

He flicked a glance at her.

"Thank you for being here."

"You already said that."

"I'm going to keep saying it."

He met her gaze. Moisture, not really tears but definitely there, welled in her eyes. "Ah, sweetheart."

She sniffed. "I'm not crying."

"Of course you aren't." He wrapped his fingers over hers where she held his arm then he leaned over to press his lips against her temple. "One step at a time, lady. We will prevail."

With a nod, her eyes closed for a moment and she leaned into him. He rubbed his chin over her hair.

His chest tightened. He *would* keep her safe. Keep her alive.

Make love with her, again and again.

"Why don't we check and see if there's anything in this copter we can use." He rubbed his cheek over her hair. "Like protein bars. Water."

"Or another gun."

"Already checked for that." He leveraged himself upwards to lean into the open door at the top of the overturned helicopter. Although he'd done a cursory check earlier, he hadn't taken the time for a deeper search.

"Maybe the real owner hid a gun under the seat or tucked it in an innocuous hidey hole." Her fingers wrapped around his ankle, keeping that contact in place.

"Maybe." He wedged his fingers behind the seat. Something small, probably of nylon material. He tugged. *Son of a bitch.* A black, nylon bag, no more than seven or eight inches in width and less than four inches in depth. "Not sure what kind of weapon that might hold, but here you go."

With her free hand, she took the bag while he turned back to finish his search of the small, cramped cabin.

"Nothing else." Half in and half out of the cockpit, he twisted to gain purchase to shove his way out. Her fingers trailed up his leg, caressed his ass before she wrapped her fingers in his belt. "Dammit, woman."

Back on the ground, his feet solid on the rooftop, he yanked her against him, threaded both hands in her hair and took her mouth with his. She responded immediately, her lips parting for his tongue. He ground his hips against her.

Dammit all to hell.

They didn't have time for this.

But he sure as hell wanted to take the time.

He eased his mouth from hers. Missed her immediately.

She gazed up at him, her eyes hooded. Careful of her bruise, he cupped her cheeks. Pressed another kiss to her lips, this one quick, then leaned his forehead against hers.

Her sigh breathed across his jaw. "I guess I should see what you've found in this bag."

With a nod, he eased back, turned her so that her side lined up to his while he kept one arm over her shoulders. He liked her nestled there, against his body. "You look, I'll keep the contact."

She rummaged for several seconds, then shot him a quick, triumphant look before pulling a small, black device from the bag. No bigger than a pager or a small cell phone, she held it to him.

A personal GPS locator, the type used to send an emergency signal to the nearest tower.

Not a weapon, but it'd sure as hell let the cavalry know where to find them.

Although with the road still out, who knew how long that might take.

He nodded once. "Turn it on."

She fumbled with it for a moment, found the switch and activated it. "Now what?"

"We wait."

"Where do you think he is?"

"Hoffman?"

"Yes. Although that's not his real name."

About what he expected. "That file you read?"

She nodded. "Roy Addison."

"Is he actually related to the Hoffmans?"

"No. I'm pretty sure he killed them in order to take on the identity of their nephew."

"To work at this hotel?" The implication filled Gavin's mind. "Is Milford behind all of this?"

"To a degree. Roy's gone rogue. According to him, Milford believes he's dead. That he died when Tommy —"

Her voice caught and she held the back of her free hand against her mouth for a moment. "Roy killed Tommy."

Another non-surprise. "How did Hoffman know to follow you here?"

"He was already here. Said Tommy had told him this was my retreat, where I go to recharge."

"That's common knowledge at the Institute. So Hoffman and Tommy were chatty before? Friends?"

"Roy said Tommy believed they were on a recruiting mission. To simply recruit me to the Milford *team*. But Roy's orders where to grab me and Tommy had a major problem with that."

"So he had to die. Why did Hoffman go rogue?"

She leaned her head back against the roof of the copter. "Because, somehow, something Tommy said convinced him I could save him."

"From?"

"Himself."

Chapter Fifteen

"OPERATION DARKWATER." Calea, her back against the roof of the overturned, small helicopter, stared out over the edge of the building, across the wet gardens of the hotel. Gavin's presence beside her, and his shields surrounding them, grounded her. Helped to keep her calm.

The GPS device they'd found less than ten minutes ago, now tucked in her jeans pocket as Gavin had insisted, also helped with the calmness thing.

"That's what was written on the outside of Roy's file. He broke in to the doctors' offices and made copies. After he supposedly died."

"And Darkwater is what?" Gavin, facing her so that he could see the stairwell door through the glass of the helicopter's nose, rubbed small circles over the top of her hand with his thumb.

"If I'm understanding the research correctly, it's a precursor for a new drug that's shown promising help in the blood disease arena. But that's reading between the lines. The research is shrouded in mystery and all that's in Roy's file are the parts relating to him."

"Roy was ill?"

"No. Not at all. At the beginning he was quite healthy, according to the file."

"You'd said he was experimented on."

"Yes. With this precursor."

"Given straight?"

"It appears so."

"How the hell did Milford get hold of it? Wouldn't that be something that's regulated?" Like that ever stopped anyone with deep pockets and no scruples.

"You'd think so. That info wasn't in the file and Roy wasn't too talkative about any of that."

"But he let you read his file?" Gavin's gaze scanned the roof area.

Calea turned to let her gaze follow his senses, his search. Straightening, she ran the tip of her tongue over her bottom lip then pulled it between her teeth. She'd *felt* his senses, *felt* him expanding to search the entire perimeter.

Wow.

He was changing. His abilities strengthening, becoming more natural by the moment.

From under her lashes, she glanced at him then let her gaze go soft, let the vision that always seemed to be right there these last few days fill her mind.

Gavin. Smiling, surrounded by a warm, golden glow, almost like the end of a summer day, when the sun hovers just on the horizon, casting its promise for an even brighter tomorrow.

Gavin. *Arms open, welcoming. Love lighting his eyes.*

She rubbed a hand over hers.

Gavin with someone else.

She still couldn't see who the woman was, but the vision had to mean he was going to make it off this rooftop. Alive. To love and be loved.

Her chest tightened and her breath caught.

Even if wasn't by her.

Dammit, neither of them were going to die on this rooftop. She'd find a way to walk away from Gavin afterwards. To a place he wouldn't find her. Sever the binds. End the obsession. Give him his life back.

Her hands clenched, she shut down the vision. Shoved it away.

They were both going to live.

Gavin's hand griped hers, hard, and she pulled her gaze to his. A frown marred his forehead. "Are you all right?"

"Fine as I can be." She turned her hand to link her fingers with his, to press their palms together.

"Okay." Worry and a hint of suspicion shadowed his eyes. "You didn't answer my question. About Hoffman letting you read his file."

"He didn't just let me read it. He insisted I read it. To understand." With her free hand, she rubbed at the tension settled at the base of her neck. "This Darkwater is what enhanced his abilities. According to the file, he's a skillful hunter and extremely good at camouflage. At flying under the radar."

"And enhanced, he's able to become invisible?"

"He's not actually invisible." How did she explain something she wasn't quite sure of herself? "After he grabbed me, you didn't see me out there, did you?"

"No. I had no idea where either of you were until you punched me." A slight layer of ire coated his voice. "That was you."

"It was a kick. And you're quite welcome."

He chuckled and warmth filled her from the inside, loosening a bit of the tightness in her chest.

"Anyway, because he does run under the radar and because he blocked my visual presence *and* our voices, it appears to be more of a suggestive skill versus an actual ability to *be* invisible."

"Like affirmations pushed outward on steroids"

"Exactly. *I am undetectable. All I touch is undetectable.*" She searched for the best way to express her jumbled thoughts. "But it's more than him simply believing. It's like, with his belief forefront in his thoughts, he can bend *your* perceptions. You see what's around him, what's behind him. But you no longer see him."

"Quite a handy skillset."

She nodded. "But he's not really invisible. If there had been anyone else there that *he* wasn't aware of, they would have been able to see him."

"So whoever he focuses on?"

"Yes. The other night, when he trashed your room, he'd focused on us not hearing him, not feeling him. And we didn't. Neither of us."

"The aberration."

"What?"

"When the two of you vanished from sight, there was an aberration in the air. Faint, barely there. I followed it until it disappeared. On your floor, after I came down the rope, I found it again. That's how I found you, in that room."

"You sensed an aberration? Felt it? You're a hunter?" *Why hadn't she known that?*

"No." Although his face remained impassive, the expression in his eyes said different. "I've just worked with a few. Picked up a few tips here and there."

No, he protested too much. People's skillsets changed, expanded with use. Roy wasn't the only one being stretched. In reality, they all grew. Everything changed. Like her suddenly, although not clearly, being able to see Gavin's future with someone else.

Heartache down that path. She shoved those thoughts aside.

Focus.

"And now, that's what you're looking for, that aber-ration." She held his gaze. "For him to try and ambush us."

"It's worked for him in the past."

"But since he can't track you, we should be safe here. Unless he decides to check the roof."

"If he's cloaked when he gets here, I'll be able to sense his presence. If he's not, I'll have a clear target."

"He wants you dead, now. He says you're in the way."

"Damn straight. And I plan to stay in his way."

I love you. How was she going to be able to walk away from Gavin?

His brows drawn down, he shot her another of those perplexed, slightly suspicious glances. Then his gaze swung back towards the stairwell door. "He's near."

Crap.

"Whatever you do, whatever happens, stay behind me."

Oh, Lord. He was going to keep himself between her and Roy. Between her and what he called the aberration.

Always protecting her.

BEHIND THE CLEAR nose of the overturned helicopter, Gavin stretched his senses out across the hotel's roof, to reach for that signature telling him Hoffman was near.

Weak, late afternoon sun poked through the heavy cloud layer stretched over the grey Pacific. Wind blew, strong enough to vibrate the small helicopter. To mix the scent of coming rain with the brine of the ocean.

Calea squatted beside him, one hand on his thigh, the other clenched in a fist. Several times earlier, intent had wavered inside her. Not about Hoffman, but about them. There, then gone, not anything he could grasp, she was too adept at blocking him.

Dammit all to hell.

Now wasn't the time to try and figure it out.

That aberration was there. Just at the edge of what he could feel. Not yet on the roof.

Still on the stairs? Heading upwards.

Gavin wrapped his fingers around the butt of his gun. His gaze followed his senses. He'd be damned if he let that son of a bitch get his hands on Calea again.

There.

His gaze locked on the stairwell door.

Something shifted. For a split second, the air sparkled in the low light, waved upwards a few inches. Settled again. Gone.

Like a damn heat mirage in the desert.

But it wasn't hot.

And this sure as hell wasn't the desert.

Hoffman.

The door had never opened. Yet now it was just easing back into its frame. As if it *had* opened a foot or more, just enough to let someone slip through, and that person had pushed it almost closed.

"He's on the roof." Gavin kept his voice low. "Stay down. Behind me at all times."

He backed with her a few feet as she slid across the main rotor mast covering to scrunch down behind it. Calea would watch his back. His focus was front and forward, at the edge of the helicopter's nose, between the fiberglass body and the rounded glass, so he could see without being a huge target himself.

Kill Dunbar.

Hoffman's intent.

Couldn't get more direct than that.

Not if I kill you, first. Gavin tamped down his thoughts. No sense risking the projection of his thoughts. Who knew what other kind of skills Hoffman had. Or had developed.

One.

Two.

Three. Gavin cupped the butt of his Sig, stood to lean against the body of the helicopter. With Calea's hand on his calf and his finger on the gun's trigger, he quickly traced the trajectory of the aberration movements.

And shot.

Once.

"Son of a bitch." Hoffman flickered into view then out again as an M1 assault rifle hit the rooftop and skittered to a stop.

The aberration shifted several feet to the left, more in front of the stairwell than out in the open, then it stopped moving. Appeared to stand still.

Gavin ducked down and pressed his hand against Calea's. Their presence might not be a secret any longer, but they still weren't going to give away her exact location. Not yet, anyway. He eased forward to watch through the glass.

Hoffman continued to flicker in and out of sight. He made no attempt to pick up the rifle. Gavin spared a quick glance at the weapon. Blood coated its wooden cradle.

He'd nailed the bastard.

Probably in the hand.

Wouldn't stop him, but might slow him down.

Gavin tested for the aberration, popped up, aimed and fired twice.

Both bullets hit the doorframe of the stairwell. He ducked again.

Shit.

He'd missed. Those bullets hadn't gone through anything but the door frame. Why had he missed? How had Hoffman gotten out of the way that fast?

A shot whizzed over the top of the helicopter, from the right. From the area where the rope lay. Followed by two more shots.

Hoffman might be injured, but he was still armed.

Gavin leaned forward to visually scan the area through the copter's nose.

Hoffman stood, visible, next to the ledge, his head up, a feral look to his dark eyes. Both hands cupped his handgun and blood dripped from the wound in his right hand. The man's mouth worked, as if he uttered silent words.

Prayers or curses. Gavin's money was on curses.

He stretched to lay on his side on the wet cement of the roof. Dampness seeped through his shirt as he aimed his Sig around the bubbled nose of the copter. With his finger light on the trigger, he sighted Hoffman.

The man disappeared.

Again.

Gavin shot twice.

The aberration moved towards the stairwell.

Shit. How the hell was he missing?

Gavin scrambled around to the front of the helicopter's nose. Calea scrambled with him. The aberration moved towards the tail. Gavin grabbed Calea's hand and pulled her to him. "He's circling."

Her face tight, she nodded and slipped behind him as the aberration stopped its forward movement.

This was a bad remake of the morning with the helicopter in place of the Hummer.

They needed a different outcome this time. They needed to smoke him out.

Gavin squatted, balancing his weight on the balls of his feet. He'd used at least half his ammunition. There wasn't any extra. There wouldn't be any reloading.

Any more shots would have to count.

"Hoffman." Gavin silently counted to three. "You're real good at hit and run, aren't you? A coward's game. You've mastered it."

Silence stretched over the waves hitting the rocks and the rising wind.

The aberration moved closer to the tail of the copter.

"Taking pot shots while you're hidden. Hitting women." Gavin motioned to Calea to ease further around nose of the helicopter. "What are you afraid of, Hoffman?"

The aberration shifted. "You're also hiding, Dunbar. Behind a flimsy helicopter."

"I'm not stupid. I can't see you."

"So I'm stupid for hiding, but you're not?" Hoffman's voice raised.

Gavin, leaning around the nose of the helicopter, spotted Hoffman's shoes under the tail. No longer invisible. "I'm not the one with two bullet holes in him."

"You should be running out of bullets soon."

"I have just enough to take you out."

"I don't think so."

"See, that's the problem, Hoffman." He kept his tone conversational. Friendly, even. "You're not thinking. All that shit in your system has messed you up. Made you dumb."

"So Calea told you about Darkwater." Hoffman squatted, his injured hand between his spread knees, dripping blood on the cement. "Then you know why I need her."

From his position Gavin still couldn't see Hoffman's face. "You're not getting her."

"I *have* to have her. You will not stop me."

"Obsession's a tricky thing. It'll eat at you until you can't think straight. Best to let it go. Move on."

"Never."

Calea's hand dropped from his back.

What the hell?

He flicked a glance towards her, but she was already moving toward the assault rifle.

"She's here." Hoffman lifted his weapon and fired. But his aim wobbled and the bullet went wide.

Gavin rolled to his right as Hoffman stood and took two steps in Calea's direction.

No. This wasn't happening. Gavin surged upwards, aimed for Hoffman's head and fired at the same time a barrage of bullets hit Hoffman's chest.

The man went down. Flat on his back, his weapon still in his lax hand. A single hole in his forehead and multiple ones across his torso.

The man was dead.

Gavin spun towards Calea.

She stood, bare feet braced apart, rifle lifted with the butt tucked against her shoulder, and the barrel pointed at Hoffman.

In less than three steps he had the rifle out of her hands and his arms wrapped tight around her. His heart pounded hard enough to come through his chest, but she was safe.

Alive.

In his arms.

"God, Calea." He pressed his lips to her forehead.

Shaking, she dipped her head and burrowed against him to press her face to his chest. "He's dead."

"Yes."

"I killed him."

"We killed him."

She nodded. "He's dead."

In the distance a soft thump-thump sounded.

The cavalry must've found another helicopter.

Chapter Sixteen

A BALMY BREEZE lifted the ends of Calea's hair, and billowed the material of her thin, filmy white bathing suit cover around her. She sat on the sun toasted sand, her legs drawn up with her heels dug into that sand and her chin on her knees. Warm Caribbean water lapped against her toes, occasionally caressing her bare feet.

For the last two months she'd made a point of catching every sunset. Of sitting here as shadows lengthened behind her and the sun bathed her face with its golden hue. Of being grateful she still had sunsets to watch.

A life to live.

Roy Addison was dead. Whether her bullets or Gavin's had killed him didn't matter. The threat was gone. The rest of life moved on.

No more could have or should haves.

No more pining for what wasn't hers any longer.

If it ever had been.

Gavin was free to live his life, now, without her as an excuse.

She hadn't had the vision since she'd slipped away from the Institute and she took that as an omen she'd made the right decision. A clean break.

And it didn't matter how much it hurt. Or that she'd wake up at night with cheeks damp from crying in her dreams. None of that mattered.

She'd made the right decision.

The breeze stilled, held its breath.

"Looks like it's going to be a beautiful sunset." Gavin's voice settled over her, caressed her skin as surely as that breeze now sighed.

"How'd you find me?" She kept her gaze on the horizon.

He squatted in front of her and balanced on the balls of his bare feet. The legs of his lightweight, off white, khakis were damp, even though there were rolled up past his ankles. "You certainly didn't make it easy this time."

"You weren't supposed to look this time."

"I know."

"Gavin, you need to leave." She squinted. The sky behind him began to change. The clouds along the horizon took on a soft, pink glow.

"Not until I have my say."

"You don't think we said all there was to be said in Oregon?"

"No." He reached down, between his knees, and drew a circle in the sand. "On that rooftop, there in Oregon, I read your intent to walk away from me."

She frowned.

"Yeah. I was surprised at that, too. At being able to read you. I've thought a lot about that, and I believe it's because you didn't have your shields up. And maybe because you were inside mine."

"I hadn't yet decided to come here, so you didn't pick that up on the rooftop."

He smiled and it arrowed straight into her heart.

Damn him.

"Turns out I do have a few hunter skills after all."

She slid a sideways glance his way. One side of his mouth lifted.

"When we finished the debriefing and you locked yourself away at the Institute, Ben said to give you time. So, I did. But then you disappeared."

She swallowed once and lifted her chin. "Obviously, I didn't disappear."

"Ben wouldn't tell me where you were. Only that you were all right. That you were safe."

"He didn't know. I didn't want him telling you."

"I understand the need for space, Calea. But your safety —"

"The threat was eliminated. Ben has the Darkwater file." Clinical. Just the facts. She'd get through this as long as she buried those damn emotions. "There's no more need to hide."

"But you are."

"I'm taking a break. Watching sunsets." *Trying to get you out of my system.*

"You left without talking to me."

"Unlike you, I believe we said all there was to say. I'm nothing more than an obsession to you. What was it you told Roy? Best to let it go. You won't, so I did."

"Calea."

"You need to get on with your life. Find someone to love."

"Are you going to do the same?" He dug a diagonal line across his circle in the sand.

"Eventually." *Never.* "Why don't you leave so I can enjoy my sunset?"

Alone.

The hollowness in her chest widened.

Why were good intentions so damn hard?

"Actually, I have found someone to love."

A lump thickened in her throat, made it hard to swallow. Orange and gold mixed with the pink and intensified the colors of the clouds along the horizon. Those glorious colors reflected in ripples over the water. She lowered her chin as she blinked back moisture. Dammit, she wasn't going to cry. Not now.

"You were right about a lot of things, Calea." He kneeled. A small wave washed up over his feet, soaking his pants up to his knees. He chuckled, then leaned forward to lift her chin with two fingers.

She stared at his chin.

"I'm not my father."

"It's good you realize that."

"And you're more than an obsession for me." He lay his hands over hers where they gripped her knees. "You're the woman I love."

She blinked. Her gaze flicked up to meet his. "You do?"

Behind him, the sunset flared in golden rays to frame him against the drama filled sky. His grin crinkled the corners of his eyes, bringing her vision to life in front of her.

Speechless, she opened her mouth only to close it again.

In a prophecy she shouldn't have been able to see, she was Gavin's future. His woman. His love.

Tears welled then spilt over her lashes but she didn't bother wiping them away.

"Tell me you love me, too, Calea Fontaine." He rocked back on his heels, pulling her with him and into his arms.

"I love you, too, Gavin Dunbar. Always."

If you enjoyed GAVIN'S WOMAN and would like to see more stories in the PSI Sentinel series, please consider leaving a review for this book with your favorite ebook seller.

Every review is appreciated.

To stay up to date with Pamela and to learn more about her upcoming releases, sign up for her newsletter: http://eepurl.com/bbOUjv

You can also visit her at the following places on the web:

www.PamelaMoran.com
www.facebook.com/pamelamoranauthor
www.goodreads.com/PamelaMoran
www.pinterest.com/pamelamoran/
Twitter: Pam_Moran

Available now:

STOLEN SPIRIT
(PSI Sentinels, Book One)

Hearing his dead ex-girlfriend's voice in an empty room is enough to make a man question his sanity. Worse is when that ex insists she shouldn't have died. Broken cop Jake Carrigan has no interest in delving into a past full of heartache and regrets. But he can't deny she still matters, even if she's simply a voice in his head.

Hannah Dixon is having a hard time believing she's dead. How can she be when she feels so much inside? She can see Jake, can talk to him, but she can't touch him. And right now, touching Jake is all she wants.

Jake's probe into Hannah's death stirs up a sinister psychic link, something dark that will stop at nothing to keep its secrets. To protect her own heart, Hannah left Jake once. Can she leave him again to protect his life?

BLIND SIGHT
(PSI Sentinels, Book Two)

Death plagues Gabe Nicholetti's dreams, but he can't save the people in his visions. The most he can do is bring their killers to justice. But this time, this victim makes it all personal.

Rily Carrigan is a dead woman, or she will be in a matter of days as her past rushes forward to shatter her carefully constructed world. But Rily doesn't believe fate is absolute. How is she going to convince the man who's seen too many die that it's possible to save her life?

Just outside a small, Oregon town, something malevolent lurks, waiting to seize what was once promised then stolen. Together, Gabe and Rily need to find a way to deny fate and keep Rily live.

ELSIE'S SECRET
(A PSI Sentinel Novella)

A PSI agent, Sebastian Alexander has secrets that once came between him and the woman he still loves. Finding her prowling around where she doesn't belong turns his simple reconnaissance into a rescue mission threatening to blow everything apart. Is he willing to risk his secrets to save her life?

Elsie Quartermaine has one goal. Save her nephew from a sadistic kidnapper. Sebastian is the one man who can help her. But divulging her secret puts more than her life in jeopardy. Can she trust Sebastian with her nephew's life? Her own? What about her heart?

As dawn creeps over the horizon, can they find enough trust in each other to stay alive?

Coming Early Summer 2015
Darkwater Echoes
PSI Sentinels: Darkwater Guardians, Book One

By Pamela Moran

Footsteps pounded across the deck above. Trent Sawyer, awake at the first thud, rolled from his berth and snatched his gun from under his pillow.

Barefoot and wearing only a black pair of shorts, he moved silently across the dark cabin to the door. He waited several heartbeats before letting the motion of a small wave hitting the side of the sailboat cover the sound of him opening the door a small fraction.

Light from the upper galley spilled through the crack and into his room.

Voices carried down to him, voices that shouldn't have been there – much less arguing over who was going to start the freaking boat's engines.

His boss' boat. Neither of those rough voices belonged to the man.

Trent wasn't letting whoever was up on deck steal _this_ boat. Not on his first night. He hadn't even been on the boat – or in Key Largo – for more than a couple hours.

Not going to happen.

With his gun leading and his body crouched low, Trent slipped into the narrow hallway. He slid one bare foot onto the bottom stair, cringed at the soft groan of weathered wood then shifted his weight to ease his other foot up another step.

On a deep exhale of breath, he lifted his head above the solid railing. Two men, one a blonde giant and the other a squat redhead, both burly and wide through the shoulders, stood across the galley with their backs to him. Their voices lower than earlier, they seemed to be arguing over a sheaf of papers they had spread over the Captain's table.

Now was as good a time as any.

Trent straightened. He aimed his gun at Blondie's head. "What the hell are you doing on my damn boat?"

Both men whipped around, their faces slack with shock.

A small amount of satisfaction welled in Trent's gut.

Mongrels, both of them.

Their eyes brightened and their mouths widened into comical grins. They started forward.

"What the –?" Pain, sharp and sudden, splintered Trent's thoughts.

His world went black.

✧ ✧ ✧

Join Pam's newsletter to stay up to date on
PSI Sentinel releases!

http://eepurl.com/bbOUjv